There Goes the Neighborhood

Jane W. Wolfinbarger

ISBN: 1470181622
ISBN-13: 978-1470181628

A CooperWolf Book

"Real life beyond imagination"

www.janewwolfinbarger.wordpress.com

For Pat, who has always believed in me and my writing.

CONTENTS

Acknowledgements

I have told myself stories for years. I have amused myself in jobs that required my hands but not my mind, I have amused my children when they were growing up, and I have amused myself whenever I was bored by telling myself stories. (The years I worked nights making donuts were great for the storytelling.)

But, until a few years ago, I didn't put any of the stories down.

I finally decided I needed to write, not just imagine, and joined an online writing group, Soul Food Cafe, which nurtured and nourished the storyteller in me. I chose to use the pen name She Wolf, and I wrote and wrote.

Somewhere along the line, I realized that I needed to write as myself, Jane, and I also realized that I wanted to write for a larger audience.

My husband, Pat, brought up the idea of e-publishing, and after mulling it over and talking with a good friend who was also writing and looking for a place to publish, I decided that e-publishing was the route I wanted to take.

I have many people I need to thank for this collection of stories and their advent into the world of books. First of all, there is my husband Pat, who has always been right there with an encouraging word or a boot to the posterior, depending on which was needed at the time. Then I need to thank my children, Lee, Peter, Lyra and Aaron, who have always thought Mom could do whatever she set out to do. I also need to thank my friends in the Saturday night group, who have helped keep my imagination lively and, again, have believed in and encouraged me. And, finally, I cannot leave out my fellow writers at the on-line writing community Soul Food Café, who saw me through my early efforts in writing, and still asked for more.

There Goes the Neighborhood

NIGHT SERVICE

The holiday visit with the relatives had been pleasant, but John was tired and ready to be home. That was why he was pushing the drive, trying to make one more town before he stopped for the night. He knew it was late, really too late to stop but too late to still be driving, but the coffee had been nice and strong at the last truck stop. He thought he had a few more miles left in him.

If only he knew what the next town was. That detour off the main highway due to what the highway patrolman said was a fatal accident left him unsure of where he actually was. All he knew was that it was a small highway running through woods covered with a thick layer of white. A gentle snow was falling, the flakes big and fluffy.

John sighed and fiddled with the GPS unit he had been given for Christmas. Apparently, he hadn't installed it correctly before he left, as after a few miles of traveling on the detour, it had gone on the fritz. A blank screen taunted him. He glanced up, but there was no traffic coming, so he leaned over and poked at the unit some more, swearing as the screen flickered and then died again.

Jake barked from the back seat. John realized he was drifting and yanked the wheel back again.

Jake whined.

"You can't have to go again," grumbled John.

Jake's response was to paw at the back door with one huge black paw and whine once more.

"Okay, fine, I'll stop. Just my luck to have a Labrador retriever with a bladder the size of a walnut." He figured he could try to find a map in the glove box while he was stopped and kill two birds with one stone.

Jake just whined again, this time more urgently.

John pulled over onto the snowy shoulder. His car had all-wheel drive so even though the snow was deep, it shouldn't be a problem to get back out. He grabbed the leash and slogged around to the passenger side door; even with no traffic, he wasn't going to let Jake out on the highway side of the car.

When he opened the door to hook the leash to Jake's collar, Jake shoved into the opening and rammed his muscular body out of the car before John could get the leash on him. Wagging ecstatically, he pranced through the snow, plowed through a drift by the trees, and stopped to water a snow covered bush. John called him, but Jake serenely ignored his master with the selective hearing of a dog happily free from his leash.

Finished, he shook himself and stood there, sniffing the breeze while John floundered towards him through knee-high drifts. John paused, too, and the world was silent in the snowy night, with the hush only freshly falling snow can bring to the world.

Then, with a happy bark, Jake broke the silence and bounded off into the brush. With a curse, John labored after him.

By the time he got through the drifts by the road and to the edge of the woods, Jake was long out of sight. His trail through the snow was plain though, and John set off resignedly after him. All those obedience lessons, and the damned dog still wouldn't come when he escaped without his leash.

Jake had taken a meandering course, but at least he managed to avoid the thickest areas of brush.

Under the trees, the snow wasn't as deep, and since John was following the path Jake had broken in the snow, he made good time following the dog. Periodically, he stopped and called for Jake, and once he heard an answering bark in distance, but Jake still refused to come.

John stopped to lean against a tree and catch his breath. The night was bright from the snow and the woods looked magical under their white coating. Here and there he could see glints of icicles hanging from branches, remnants of a brief thaw just before this storm had hit. The air was completely silent and John could hear his own heart pounding in the stillness. He hummed a few bars of Silent Night – the song was made for a night like this one, still and peaceful and snowy.

Finally Jake's trail led to what must be a small road - a ribbon of deep snow running under the extended arms of the trees overhead. It was unused, though, with the snow on it pristine but for Jake's tracks.

Sighing, John slogged on down the road, calling Jake again. At least he didn't have to worry about tripping over rocks and roots in the middle of a road. In the distance, he could hear Jake barking again and picked up his pace. He really hoped the dog wasn't barking by someone's house and waking them up.

John followed Jake's path off the road again and down a small path. The trees and bushes here looked as though they had been tended once upon a time – although that time was clearly long ago. Jake had leaped over a low stone wall here, but John found a rusty gate and pushed it open, creaking, through the snow. He saw Jake right away, standing by a grove of trees and wagging, a big doggy grin on his face and his tongue hanging out the side of his mouth.

John walked over to him and snapped the leash on an unresisting Jake and then paused to look around. The snow was getting lighter and a full moon was starting to glow behind the clouds. It lit up the area so that John could get a good look. Drifts of snow in long lines with right angles suggested the existence of low walls or perhaps the ruins of a building. Bare, snowy trees and the low round mounds of snowed-over bushes at intervals suggested a garden, perhaps. The grove of trees that Jake had paused beside was made up of huge old giants, closely planted in a line about forty feet long.

Jake pulled the leash suddenly and, caught off balance, John stumbled behind him through the line of trees.

There was another line, planted on the other side about twenty feet away, and at either end there was still more of the majestic forest elders. John was no naturalist, and had no idea what sort of trees they might be, but they were clearly big and old. Their branches laced overhead to form a vaulted roof over the space. At one end there was an opening while at the other end was a small, snow covered hummock with bushes on it. John could tell that the ground under his feet must be carpeted by a smooth coat of green grass in the summer – it would be a lovely place. Here, too, evidence of a recent slight thaw had left icicles hanging from some of the branches, particularly at the end where the leafless bushes were. With the sun on it, the scene would be stunning. As it was, it was magical and peaceful.

John was put in mind of a chapel, made of nothing but what grew naturally. The effect was heightened by the small drifts of snow that had blown between the gaps of the trees into lines that looked like pews running up and down the length of the space.

John – and apparently Jake, too – felt like he was intruding into a sacred space of some sort and together they turned to quietly walk back between the trees. As they stepped through the gap, though, John heard a noise. It sounded like the rusty gate being pushed open and someone walking to the end of the grove closest to the gate. He turned to see who was coming in.

"Who's there?" he meant to say, but nothing came out. He tried to move, but he couldn't. Jake sat at his feet, unmoving as a black statue, snowflakes spotting his fur.

As John watched, an elderly woman came into view. John's most immediate concern was that she wasn't dressed for the weather. She wore a light house dress and a sweater over it. Her feet were clad in fluffy scuffs that had seen better days. She hummed an old tune – something from the big band era, John thought, as she wandered down the center of the tree-space. Again he tried to say something, but no sound came out. Was this fear? What was happening to him, he wondered.

As John began to panic over his paralysis and inability to speak, there were more sounds coming in from the area of the gate. Slowly, more people entered the vaulted space. An elderly man shuffled in who was as under dressed as the old woman, a couple bundled up with blankets around their shoulders entered together, and a man with ice skates draped over his shoulders came in. A teenage girl came in, dragging a huge inner tube of the sort that kids used to slide down hills; she left the tube at the back. It was soon joined by a pair of skis propped there by man and a sled brought in by a boy of ten or so. A slightly older boy came in. He was followed by a couple in snowmobile suits.

A toddler came in, crying, clad only in a diaper and t-shirt; the old woman who had come in first went to him and picked him up and comforted him. A few more people entered, but the stream of them was slowing down. The space was nearly full now. Time seemed to pause, and the people in the area were as silent as the night was. They seemed to be waiting for something. Still they milled around a bit, seeming to mingle and visit with one another, albeit very quietly.

Then John heard one last group of people approaching. A man and woman finally came in, accompanied by a small boy and girl. They looked bewildered, and as John studied them, he realized that they were covered with blood and what looked like fatal wounds. It dawned on him that many of the people there didn't look right, somehow. How he had missed it at first, he didn't know. The neck of the girl with the inner tube was at an odd angle. The man with skis had a huge dent in his forehead. The man with skates was wet, as was one of the boys. And each of them, every one, was pale. John swallowed as he realized that it was the pallor of death. The group of mostly silent people, the horrible injuries some of them had, their paleness – they were almost blue in the snowy light – what was going on here? Where were all of the dead coming from and why were they coming here? And why was he here, watching all of this?

His heart racing, John tried desperately once again to move, but it was no use. He just couldn't. John had always seen himself as a man's man, never giving in to fear. The sensation of being unable to move was completely foreign to him – even in his dreams he was never paralyzed with fear.

If he could have run, John would have. If he could even have slipped away, out of sight behind a tree, John would have. But he couldn't so much as twitch a finger.

He was stuck here in a gap in the line of trees, hoping beyond hope that no one would look his way. So far, by some miracle, they hadn't. He shuddered to think what might happen, or what it might mean, if they did.

One of the men, a hunter by his clothing, came over to the newcomers and said, "Welcome. We were waiting for you." He added kindly, "It will be all right now."

Then the people stopped milling around and slowly began to go toward the lines of snow – the ones that looked like pews in a church – and began to stand in them. John thought that his heart would beat out of his chest as the pale dead people filed into lines beside him.

Strangely, not one of them looked at him. He might have been one of the trees and Jake a bush for all the notice they gave him.

Now the tree-chapel was full and silent. A small breeze came up, rustling the branches of the icicle-laden bushes at the front, causing the icicles to strike each other. And each time they struck, it sounded like a bell was chiming. Soon a small carillon was playing.

Then, on the little hill amidst the bells of the icicles, a form slowly appeared. It was shadowy and dark up there, but John could swear that he saw huge wings spreading over the whole area.

The clouds parted and the moon shone through the branches lighting the area. The people within it were swaying gently to the music. John noted with terror that he could almost see through many of them.

Somewhere nearby, a bell tolled. Twelve times it rang. John found himself wondering if it was a real bell or the ghost of one.

Then, as the bell finished ringing, with the moon shining into the front and center of the space just in front of the little hill, the form on the hill spoke.

"It is time," it said in a pure, clear voice.

A ball of light formed in the moonlit spot and grew until it was the height of the tree branches above and several feet wide.

"Come," said the voice, and the first of the people filed forward. It was the old woman, carrying the toddler.

John had a brief flash to a headline glimpsed sometime on his holiday visit, "Elderly Woman Wanders Away During Storm – Family Distraught." And then another one he didn't remember seeing but somehow knew, "Toddler Found Frozen After Long Search."

The old woman put the toddler down and took him by the hand, leading them firmly into the light. It flared around them, and John though he could see their bodies melt away, replaced by glowing forms of light. One by one, each of the people did the same, approaching the light joyfully.

As each of them passed into the light, John's mind filled with headlines and stories: a boy drowned when he fell through the ice of a pond, a skier who skied into a tree, snowmobilers lost, an accident on an icy road. Images flashed in his mind, and he knew that he hadn't read all of these stories, yet he felt as if he must have. Everyone there had a story, and now John knew them all.

The last ones in line were the family that had come in late. They clung together, hesitating fearfully. The voice behind the light spoke again, "You are so new you have had no chance to adjust and accept. Please trust in me and enter with the others. You will understand then."

Slowly, trembling, the family approached the light. In his mind, John saw a car wrecked beyond all hope on the road he had taken the detour from, and understood why they were so confused.

They walked slowly into the light, and then, with bodies now glowing with light themselves, they leapt joyfully beyond and out of sight.

The light still shone there, but all of the people were gone. John wondered what it was waiting for. Then he thought of driving down the road, and the GPS. Could the light be waiting for him?

Was he paralyzed with fear, or with death? But the others, they had all been able to move, and he still couldn't. He tried again but still nothing worked.

Then the light finally began to shrink. It became a ball once more and then faded out of sight.

His eyes full of the light, John could only see the figure on the hill as a vague shape, and he waited to see if it would address him. Still nothing happened. The silence was complete, and snowflakes started to drift down slowly once more. With a noise like a sigh, the figure on the hill seemed to fold its wings and then slowly faded away.

A wind came up, swirling the snow like wings passing by in the tree-room and whispering in John's ear: "Done." And then, "And Witnessed."

Jake raised his head and let out a long, mournful howl that reverberated to John's very core, and he heard his own heart answering it. He would have lifted his head and howled, too, if he could. He felt tears tracking down his face; whether they were from fear he had felt, relief that he had not been one of those entering the light, sadness that he wasn't one of them, or sorrow that the stories of those who left were done, he didn't know.

And then, suddenly he could move again.

Jake could too, and tugged John back towards the gate. John noticed in passing that his and Jake's were the only footprints that he could see anywhere.

The walk back to the car was completed in silence; even the usually ebullient Jake was subdued. He jumped quietly back into the car and curled in a ball, falling asleep immediately as only a dog can do.

John entered the car more slowly. He glanced at the GPS, which was cheerfully displaying a map now, and turned the thing off. He rummaged in the glove box for a map, which he carefully studied before pulling the car back out onto the empty, snowy road. He didn't think he wanted to attend another meeting like tonight's, not in any form.

Jane W. Wolfinbarger

PLUMBING AND THE MODERN NECROMANCER

When the doorbell rang in the middle of the night, all Alison Gates could say was, "Thank God." She pulled her dressing gown belt tighter and yanked the door open. "Thank God you're here. It's this way! Hurry up!" The handsome young man dressed in a black uniform and standing in the doorway holding the box of tools stared after her but didn't move. She turned and snapped, "Aren't you going to come in? Hurry up, I said. The damn thing is leaking like a waterfall and the bathroom is already soaked!"

The man smiled slightly, hefted his tools and then stepped into the house. "Right away, Ms. Gates," he replied as he followed her to the basement.

Half an hour later, as the plumber finished replacing the leaking section of pipe in the basement bathroom ceiling, Alison peered into the bathroom. She was now clad in yoga pants and a sweatshirt, which the plumber thought was a pity. He had rather liked the dressing gown look.

"Thank you SO much for coming so quickly – and in the middle of the night, too, ah – I don't think I caught your name?"

"It's Laddie, and you're welcome. It's Northern Lights Plumbing's specialty – those middle of the night emergencies. Our motto is, 'We're up all night so you don't have to be.' We also specialize in sewer and septic tank problems." He smiled briefly and she caught a glimpse of very white teeth.

"Well, Laddie, I'm still very grateful. I'd have had a hell of a mess to clean up otherwise. Do I pay you, or does your company send a bill?"

"We'll bill you. No problem."

"Great. Now, can I offer you something to drink before you go? Some cocoa or something?"

Laddie winced slightly and thanked her, but, "I don't think so. I don't like sweets. However, if you don't mind, a glass of water?" He looked at her and she gazed into his eyes, which were so very, very deep…

A little while later, Laddie loaded up his truck, whistling, while Alison Gates finished rinsing out the water glass in the kitchen. This company was so very nice - the plumbers were prompt, efficient, and this one had been positively dreamy he was so good looking! She'd have to call them again, and she'd certainly recommend them to her friends.

As she got ready to climb back into her bed, she scratched irritably at the mosquito bite on her neck. Well, that was new. One of the little nuisances must have gotten in when she was opening the door for Laddie-the-plumber. Funny how tired she was, all of a sudden. She shrugged and smiled and fell right asleep.

The next morning, shortly before dawn, Laddie slapped the paperwork from the night before on his boss's desk and smiled, showing all of his teeth. Some of them were very sharp and rather frightening.

"You got a call last night, Vlad? Good. You were looking a little bit peaked. It had been a while, no?" the man behind the desk was well into middle age, but tall and fit looking. He also looked like someone not to be trifled with. "You had better hurry, though. It's going to be dawn in a little bit and you really don't want to have to hide in the trunk of your car again."

He reached for the paperwork. "What's this? Extra?" Nicholas Northing, necromancer, founder and owner of Northern Lights Plumbers raised an elegant eyebrow.

Laddie, or Vlad, as Nicholas had called him, smiled again. "Yep. I'll have that amount transferred to your offshore account before I go to bed for the day. This one was SO worth it.

"You know, when you first approached us with this idea, I was skeptical, but now – now I think it was a touch of genius. For those of us who are tired of the club scene, this is perfect! All I have to do is a little plumbing, and I've got an endless buffet. And tonight's customer, ah, yes, she was extraordinary. Elegant, beautiful – all of the extras. She was the equivalent of a four–star restaurant." He sighed at the memory. "Oh yes, I've decided not only am I happy to pay for the privilege of working for Northern Lights Plumbing, I'm going to help you open those branches in Chicago and St. Louis you've been talking about. I'll talk to my family and friends and I'll get back to you tomorrow night. After I pay a little call to Ms. Gates and see how the plumbing is holding up." Laddie left, still smiling.

Nicholas smiled, too. He entered the information Laddie had given him in a specially encrypted file and shredded the paperwork. It had been an excellent day when he had decided to open the plumbing company using zombies as the plumbers and a better one still when he decided to hire vampires for the night shift. The vampiric night crew were invited into houses where they could have a discreet meal when their work was done, and they paid HIM for the privilege of working for a legitimate company that gave them that opportunity. It was a win-win situation, and he liked that. And, he thought as he entered the billing information into the computer for Alison Gates, nothing like getting paid twice for one service call.

Even the regular day shift was more than profitable. Zombies didn't require pay, and the bank accounts his "employees" had set up were actually just feeders into his untraceable off-shore accounts. A few carefully placed concealment spells and no one would ever be the wiser. It had been the start of something very good when he had finally perfected that high-level re-animation spell.

Nicholas spun around in his desk chair and settled down to do some paperwork. Barbara at the front desk had left him a note - one of the zombies that worked the day shift needed his anti-decomposition spells renewed. Fortunately, the apprentice – or rather supervisor on the job – had been able to explain away the odd odor by suggesting it was lingering on the plumber's boots from an earlier job, but that kind of thing just wasn't acceptable in a business. He made a list of the things he would need for the spell and went to the cold-storage locker to find the zombie with the B.O. problem.

That evening, Nicholas adjusted his bow tie ever so slightly and brushed non-existent lint off of his tailored tuxedo. He offered the lovely young woman with him his arm. "Are you ready, my dear? I think they're waiting on us."

Nicholas was the guest of honor at this banquet. He was accepting the award for Businessman of the Year – the success of Northern Lights Plumbing was astonishing everyone. Everyone, that is, except Nicholas. Each bit of that success was planned and gloated over, and this award was simply the public agreeing with Nicholas.

As soon as he entered the room a pompous man in a rent-a-tux accompanied by a woman in an elderly evening gown accosted him. "Mr. Northing, I'm Mayor Peters, and I want to congratulate you on your award. And I have a special surprise for you tonight…." The mayor paused as the woman with him elbowed him in the side. She smiled at Nicholas and batted her eyes. The man choked for a moment and then said, "Oh my, mustn't say too much. I just wanted to warn you not to take off after your award." He hurried off, towed by the woman who looked back at Nicholas and winked.

"All right, then, let's find our seats," Nicholas pulled his date, who was scowling after the woman, to the table. "I suppose we'll find out what all of that is about later."

At the end of the banquet, he did. Right after he was presented with his award, the mayor came forward again. "Mr. Northing, our fair city has noticed the good you have been doing. Contributions to the city beautification fund, the establishment of the Northing Fund for Afterschool Care, the new additions to the senior center – none of this has been missed by the watchful eyes of the public. Tonight, we, the city, would like to acknowledge your contributions and honor you with these, the Keys to the City!"

Nicholas smiled, posed, made a lovely acceptance speech, and pretended to be utterly overcome with pleasure. He was mildly surprised – he hadn't expected this sort of thing quite yet. Apparently these people were easier to impress than he had thought. He spent the rest of the night with various women all vying for his attention and his date quietly seething and baring her teeth at them. Nicholas enjoyed himself immensely.

The morning newspaper had a front page photo of him holding his plaque for businessman of the year and the symbolic oversize gold-plated keys. Nicholas smiled once again and had Barbara at the desk clip a copy for framing.

Shortly after lunch, Nicholas became aware of a fracas in the front office. It was loud, but he had every confidence that Barbara could handle it. She was formidable and even Laddie kept his distance from her no matter how attractive he thought she was. This time, however, whatever it was overcame even Barbara's best defenses. A knock sounded on his office door, and Barbara, looking frazzled and annoyed, poked her head in.

"Mr. Northing, I'm sorry sir, but these men just won't take no for an answer. I told them they needed an appointment to see you, but they said they didn't, and they wouldn't leave, and well, frankly sir," here her voice dropped so low he could barely hear her, "I'm afraid they'll scare off anyone else who comes in. One of them smells a bit like the boys when they've been on a sewer job and their spells are failing, all at the same time."

She twisted her head around to peek at the office behind her, and then suddenly she jerked the door open and almost tumbled inside. A bright flash of light lit up the room at the same time.

Barbara stood up straight, gasped slightly, and said, "Um….right. He's right in here, gentlemen."

She sailed out of the room, leaving the door open behind her. Nicholas raised his eyebrows, intrigued at whatever could have ruffled Barbara's feathers.

Three men strode into the room, followed by another, much younger fellow who didn't stride. He scuttled. The first three men were older, and two of them were quite unkempt. The fourth man seemed to be possessed of several nervous ticks. Given the identity of the first three men, Nicholas really didn't blame him.

"Gregory, Malachi, Harold, please come in. It's always a pleasure to see you. And who is this fine young man?" Nicholas offered the young man the handshake that he avoided with the other three.

"Joshua, sir. I'm Gregory's apprentice." The young man barely avoided squeaking when he talked and his Adam's apple bobbed as he swallowed nervously. His hands were cold and sweaty.

"Let's not waste time on formalities, Nicholas. You know why we're here!" The oldest member of the group, who was wearing what looked like a moth-eaten bathrobe over greenish tuxedo pants, confronted Nicholas boldly. His white hair stuck out on end all over his head and his beard was of the sort that been made famous by ZZ Top several decades ago. Nicholas got a whiff of mothballs as the man moved; apparently they hadn't been as effective as they should have been in the case of the robe, since it was more holes than fabric. "We saw that photo of you in the paper!"

"Wonderful!" Nicholas beamed at the group and perched on the edge of his desk.

The next oldest member of the group interrupted, "You must cease and desist this commercial enterprise immediately. You are bringing a bad name to necromancers everywhere!" He puffed self-righteously into his moustache and straightened his double-breasted pin-striped blazer with an angry twitch.

The last member of the group, a very chubby, balding man, who was obviously the one who had offended Barbara's sense of smell, said in a trembling voice, "Really, Nicholas, this isn't dignified. How could you? I mean, a business? Necromancers intimidate, they rule, they trample over people, but they don't run a business." He shifted and some dirt sifted off his clothes onto the carpet.

Nicholas regarded them for a moment and then quirked an eyebrow at the young man who was trying to hide behind them. "What, Joshua, nothing to add?"

The second man, whom Nicholas had addressed as Malachi, snarled, "He'll stay silent as befits a good apprentice. OUR apprentices are well-behaved, unlike those hooligans you employ."

"I would prefer that you call them supervisors." Nicholas turned his back on the group and walked slowly over to his desk chair and then seated himself in a leisurely manner. He smiled slightly, said, "Just a moment," and took a cell phone out of his pocket. He fussed with it for a few moments while the group standing in the middle of the office silently fumed. Then he looked up and said, "Thank you. I just needed to confirm an appointment someone made. Northern Lights Plumbing now has an app for that." He smiled broadly.

"So, gentlemen, you came to tell me to stop running my very profitable business and go back to being a necromancer of the sort that you think I should be? Tell me, Gregory," and he turned to the man in the moth-eaten robes, "How is your house in the country? Still falling down around your ears? Didn't I hear a rumor that they shut off your electricity last fall? Winter was a bit cold, wasn't it? And you've taken on an apprentice, too. Another mouth to feed." Nicholas tsk-tsked at the older man who shuffled his feet uncertainly.

"And Harold," he turned to the rotund man dropping bits of soil on the carpet, "are you still digging up your own corpses? Do you remember who posted bond for you last time you got caught? Hmmm? There are better – and less obvious – ways to get bodies to work on, you know, in this day and age. And those animation spells you use! All they produce are shambling, rotting hulks that drop bits of themselves everywhere! And you dare talk to me about undignified behavior!"

Harold cringed and looked at the floor.

"And lastly, Malachi." Here Nicholas paused and stared at the man in the pinstriped suit and fedora. "I know who instigated this little visit."

Malachi bared his teeth and started to reply, but Nicholas kept on going, "You made your fortune running rum in the 1920's, as I recall. How DARE you condemn me for running a business! Mine, at least, is legal!"

"Yes, but at least I didn't use zombies and vampires to do it!" Malachi snarled back.

"That was a lack of foresight on your part. It's much cheaper when you don't have to pay your employees," Nicholas retorted.

"Clearly, your sort of necromancy is SO successful in this century. Thanks to movies and trite television shows, everyone thinks what we do is nothing more than special effects. Nothing scares them except no bars on their cell phone screens. Intimidation, ptahh! Look at you. All of you. Now, if there's nothing further…"

He made a small motion with his fingers and the group started moving to the door. Widened eyes suggested that they weren't moving of their own volition.

They grumbled and scuffled noisily, but were soon propelled out through door into the outer office. He could hear Barbara wishing them a good day. Suddenly the door opened again, and the young apprentice peered in. "Sir, how DID you get started in business?" he whispered hoarsely.

Nicholas looked up from his computer. "You know they are going to leave without you," Nicholas told him.

The young man waved a set of keys at him. "No they aren't. None of them can drive." He smiled slightly for the first time.

Nicholas grinned broadly back. There was hope for this young man yet, Gregory's apprentice or no. "I came into ownership of a small mortuary a few years ago. As I told Harold, there are better ways of ensuring a supply of bodies than digging up graves. I was perfecting my signature high-level animation spell on a man who had been a plumber in life. About the time I animated him, the sink sprang a leak. He got right up, went over, fixed the sink and said, 'Will that be all, sir?' And with that, an idea was born."

"Wish I were your apprentice, sir. Things are even worse than you think. Even Master Malachi's in bad straits. His mansion got foreclosed on last winter and he spent it with Master Gregory and me. And then Harold moved in with his, um, minions as he calls them." Joshua said, shuddering. "Smelly things. That was the one advantage of not having heat last winter – they didn't smell quite so much. Well, I better get that lot back home. They tend to attract a lot of attention here in town. And I don't want to deal with that."

He left, and Nicholas sat at his desk, gazing at his watch. "Three, two, one…" he muttered. Then he jumped to his feet and raced out to the parking lot, where Gregory and Malachi were trying to haul Harold into a black van by his arms. Rotund Harold was trying to climb in, but it just wasn't working. Dirt was flying off his clothing in clouds as he struggled to get his legs up. The apprentice was pushing on his posterior, vainly trying to help.

"Gentlemen, a moment please," Nicholas called. Harold turned to look at him, and Malachi and Gregory peered out of the van door curiously.

"I have a proposition for you. Take your time to consider it, but I'll need an answer by the end of the week," he began. "I am thinking of opening branches in St. Louis, Kansas City and Chicago. I could really use experienced necromancers to head up those divisions. I was considering sending my senior apprentices … Er, I mean supervisors, but there would be much traveling involved for me, and that just isn't to my taste. I wonder if any of you would be interested. You would, of course, get a portion of the profits of the branch you managed…."

The three necromancers were silent. Nicholas could see their eyes sliding to each other. The apprentice was behind them, with his eyes squeezed shut and his fingers crossed on both hands.

"Well…"

"We might…"

"How much of a share were you talking about?" Malachi snapped.

The apprentice opened his eyes and smiled.

When Nicholas went back inside after promising to bring the paperwork out to Gregory's house later in the week, Barbara stopped him. "Sir, you SO have to teach me that spell to make people leave. Last week I had a skeezy plumbing parts salesman in here hitting on me for over an hour when you were out at lunch, and nothing I could do to get rid of him worked. He finally left when your car pulled up." She shuddered.

Nicholas raised his eyebrows slightly at the idea of any mere mortal with the audacity to brave the formidable Barbara's wrath. The man must have had a death wish.

Nicholas was feeling quite generous at the moment and Barbara really was very capable, magically speaking – not to mention lovely and loyal. "Of course, my dear. Right after work!"

He hummed as he closed his office door. His plans were moving along swimmingly. As he seated himself at his desk he shivered slightly. It was suddenly a bit cold in the office. He pushed the intercom button.

"Barbara, did you do anything to the thermostat?"

"No, sir," came the reply. "Your office is set at the same temperature it always is."

"Then did anyone go back to the cold storage area?"

"No, sir. No one has come in except the visitors that you just sent on their way."

"Thank you, Barbara." He sat back and looked around. It was so cold now that his breath was coming out in little plumes. He looked again. There was an area of deeper shadow in the corner of the room.

As he gazed at it, it moved and a voice came out of the air.

"So, your erstwhile contemporaries have come to lodge a complaint, have they? Lot of losers, all of them. They never were very good and they'll certainly never amount to anything now." The voice was deep and dark and rather chilling. Nicholas shuddered slightly in spite of himself. He had never known the name that went with the voice, had never had a face to put with it, but it had haunted his nightmares for years, ever since his single previous encounter with it. He had his suspicions as to the identity of the owner, but proof was elusive. He thought of it as the Rival Necromancer, or just the Rival.

"What do you want?" he snapped uneasily.

"I just wanted to see for myself exactly what it is that you've managed to accomplish," the voice oozed. "And I have seen. While I must agree with some of your sentiments, I also think that your former fellows have a few points too."

The voice paused and the shadow grew larger, taking over an entire quarter of the room, almost to the edge of Nicholas' desk. "I want you to know, Nicholas, that I know what your game is. I know what you're doing and why you're doing it. And I want to warn you that it might be in your best interests to stop. Not all of your fellow necromancers are silly fools like those three."

The darkness moved again, circling the desk with Nicholas left in an empty area in the middle.

Despite his bravado, Nicholas was sweating while his breath puffed out in clouds in the cold.

"Yes, indeed," the voice echoed all around him, "I know what you're trying to do. And I suggest that you stop before you're gone any farther, or I shall be forced to take matters into my own hands. The power game is not one to be played lightly." Abruptly, the cloud of darkness was gone, the cold was gone, and Nicholas was left sitting at his desk.

After breathing deeply and composing himself for a few moments, he sat up straight, narrowed his eyes and said to the empty room, "We'll see about that. We'll just see about that." He turned to his computer and rapidly began composing an e-mail.

A few months later the newest branch offices were opened, the trio of necromancers were placed in charge after some (at least in Harold's case) re-training in the art of animating zombies, and Nicholas began to plan a campaign for the state house. His life was going as scripted, and he was delighted. There were no more threatening visits from black clouds and the Rival Necromancer, and slowly the bad taste in his mouth from that encounter faded.

He was at his desk one morning dealing with the small matter of a zombie who had lost a finger while working. The family's dog had found it and been growling over it happily when the lady of the house had noticed. It had taken the supervisor in charge some time and effort and a small spell to convince the woman that she had actually seen a chicken wing left over from the plumber's lunch and not an errant digit. Now Nicholas was putting a protocol in place for checking for loose fingers and so forth on a daily basis. After all, zombies couldn't feel it when a finger was about to detach after a rough job. The zombie in question would be transferred to another branch where his nine-fingered status wouldn't be remarked on.

The phone rang, and Malachi's voice came through. "Nicholas, we have an emergency here and you are the only one who can deal with it. Quite a few of the spells on the zombies in my branch are failing and I just don't know what is going on" Malachi sounded quite stressed, not at all like his usual arrogant self. "Nicholas, I know you're busy, but please, I really need your help as soon as possible." Malachi hung up before Nicholas could answer him, and didn't answer when he tried to call the man back.

Northing was on the road an hour later. He really didn't mind traveling for work, no matter what he told his staff. A fine car certainly made driving a pleasure, he thought to himself as his classic sports car hummed down the highway.

It was nearly dusk and he was an hour from his destination when the cramps started.

Nicholas was seldom ill. A lifetime – or, more accurately, several lifetimes – of working with the dead had given him an unparalleled immune system. And stomach ailments just didn't happen to him, so he was taken completely unaware by the sudden gripping pain in his gut. Sweat breaking out on his face, he drove on. Certainly whatever this was would pass quickly, and anyway he was almost to his hotel.

But the pain did not let up; the miles that had been whizzing by began to creep, and by the time Nicholas saw the sign for the rest stop, he was driving almost doubled over and was desperate to find a men's room.

He screeched into the parking lot, and hoping beyond hope that he could make it inside in time, jumped from his car and raced into the restroom. Miraculously, the place was empty despite the many cars in the parking lot.

Somewhere in the recesses of Nicholas' mind he thought that the vacant men's room was for the best; this might not be pleasant for bystanders and there were no doors on the stalls.

He had no idea.

As Northing sat in the cinder-block cubby with his arms pressed over his tormented gut, a coldness began to gather around him. At first he thought it was just another side effect of his upset stomach, but when the sweat on his forehead actually began to freeze, he knew that it wasn't that simple. He opened his eyes and when he saw the cloud of darkness gathering just outside the stall he slowly closed them again.

"So, this was a trap," he said to the darkness.

"Yes, I knew that someday I would need to eliminate you. But to do this I needed for you to come into my sphere of influence. And since you weren't coming as quickly as I wanted, I arranged for a summons. Malachi was touchingly loyal to you – he really didn't want to make that call. He said something about 'over his dead body,' so I obliged him. Those high level animation spells you've developed really are useful, aren't they? That apprentice of yours I acquired last week was so helpful when I pressed him about them. I didn't have to hurt him much at all! When I used the spells on Malachi, he sounded just like his miserable self!"

The cold edged closer as the Rival continued. "Just so you know, Malachi screamed beautifully before he died. And he'll make a very useful zombie. I always did want to take Malachi down a notch or two." He laughed.

"You know, I thought that it would be a nice touch – poetic, even – to have you die in a public toilet. The plumbing entrepreneur, dying in a toilet. I'll warm your body back up and they'll think it was a simple heart attack. Hah!" The darkness moved closer, the oily blackness creeping over Northing's toes. He could feel them starting to ache with the cold.

"The best part is, I'll be able to claim your body, too. You'll make a wonderful zombie. I think I'll let you rot a bit first, and you can become the sort of zombie you refused to create, dropping stinking pieces of yourself everywhere until you're nothing but a dirty skeleton." The Rival Necromancer's voice descended into a vicious hiss.

The darkness was all the way to Northing's knees now, but at least the searing cold distracted him from the pain in his gut.

As the darkness edged nearer, Nicholas fumbled his cell phone out of his pocket. Through the dark cloud, he could see the form of a man appearing. "I see you didn't want to just leave this up to your servant, here," he grated as the cloud pushed up against his chest.

"No, I wanted to be here in person for this one," the Rival replied. "I did warn you, you know. All you had to do was stop what you've been doing and join your fellows in obscurity. And leave the power game to me."

The cold was sucking the breath – and the life – out of him. Choking, Nicholas peered down at the cell phone in his numbing hand. He thumbed through the pages and then pressed an application.

The cell phone was plucked from his hand and flew across the restroom to the man standing there. "Ah, ah, ah….no calling for help!" the Rival Necromancer scolded, slipping the phone in his pocket.

Back in the office, an icon lit up on Barbara's computer screen. Across the country, dozens of supervisors' phones buzzed, and the same icon lit up. Everyone stopped what they were doing, pressed the corresponding application, and began chanting. Barbara's fingers danced over her computer screen at the same time, and magic flowed through cyberspace, all channeled into the cell phone now resting in the Rival Necromancer's pocket. It began to vibrate, but he didn't notice.

"Finish it!" the Rival Necromancer hissed at the darkness, and the cloud moved closer, starting to ooze its way into Nicholas' mouth and nose. He gagged, coughed and tried to pull in a breath, but nothing went into his lungs but the blackness. He was starting to turn blue and his sight was dimming. His hope was dimming, too. Something should have happened by now.

The sun finally slipped down behind the horizon, and Laddie the vampire awoke with a strange buzzing coming from his pocket. He groaned when he recognized the annoying vibration as his phone, and he pulled it out, squinting at the screen in the darkness of his coffin. When he realized what was on it, he jerked fully awake, cursed loudly, and immediately added his little bit of magic to the mix flowing through the ether.

On the verge of passing out, Nicholas could hear a mad cackle of delight from the Rival and he thought, "Must hang on…almost…hurry…"

Then the world exploded.

Or, to be more accurate, the Rival Necromancer exploded. Well, he didn't explode so much as he just vaporized. One moment he was there, the next moment there was a dull boom of air rushing into the space where he had been as trash and debris from the floor flew around the restroom. The black cloud was gone along with its master, and Nicholas gratefully sucked in a huge lungful of air.

His stomach didn't hurt anymore, the freezing cold was gone, and he could breathe. He sat there for a moment, gasping and regaining his composure. Then he remarked conversationally to the spot where the Rival Necromancer had stood, "You, know, you really should have embraced technology. It's very, very useful. Attacked by a magical rival? I have developed the perfect app for that. Applications are SO useful." He chuckled wheezily.

Northing got some stares as he returned to his coupe. One woman asked, "Are you all right mister? We heard a lot of noise in there."

Nicholas smiled his famous thousand-watt smile that always made the ladies melt. "I'm fine, thank you ma'am. Just a little bit of traveler's upset tummy." He winked and added, "Might want to let it air out in there a bit before anyone goes in." She giggled and several of the men guffawed, while Nicholas climbed into his car.

He rummaged through the glove box for his back-up phone, which was already ringing.

"Yes, Barbara," he answered. "Yes, I'm fine, and that last little bump in the road has been smoothed out. Thankfully, everything worked perfectly. Oh, and I think tomorrow we can go public with the 'purchase' of our chain of electrical shops from our dummy company, don't you?

"And then next month, the moving company and perhaps the month after the painters?" He smiled. "Please schedule me a meeting with that fellow in Hollywood about the film studio. We really need to keep those zombie and vampire movies coming. It definitely helps to keep the public oblivious to what's actually happening around them. You know, if they think of zombies and vampires as the stereotypes we promote with the media they'll never suspect that they're all around." He chuckled. "Misdirection is such a useful tactic."

Humming, he disconnected the call and pulled out onto the highway. In six months he would be recognized as the wealthiest man in the region, and within a year, the country. And that was without the offshore accounts ever coming to light - which they wouldn't, thanks to his carefully designed spells.

There was work to do; he was going to have to replace Malachi and the unnamed apprentice that the Rival Necromancer had taken out. But for now he allowed his mind to float along in a pleasant reverie. When he was President…ah, but that was just the start. He drove away, mulling over the future he had been planning for a very, very long time.

Yes, there was more than one way to have zombies take over the world. And Nicholas Northing was just the necromancer to do it.

Jane W. Wolfinbarger

SQUIRRELS IN THE ATTIC

Janice finished tying her running shoe and sat back up on the park bench, stretching. She really needed to finish her run, but she was so tired this morning it was a real push. That damned squirrel had been running around in the attic half the night. And when she finally fell asleep, she had the strangest dreams. She woke up feeling more tired than when she fell asleep.

Just a few more minutes on the bench and she'd get back to her run. In the meantime, the park was beautiful. Birds were singing, squirrels were scampering around in the trees, which was the right place for them, and kids were shrieking with joy on the playground. Someone was playing Frisbee with their dog. That guy in the blue car in the parking lot was hot – and was he looking at her?

Janice thought about her running outfit – baggy green shorts, old orange t-shirt and scruffy pony-tail - and her face burned. He probably thought she looked like a clown in this get-up. And he was very, very nice to look at. She always looked dorky for the hot ones. The circles under her eyes from lack of sleep didn't help, either. Embarrassment catapulted Janet off of the bench and she pelted off with energy she didn't realize she had.

Agent Roland James watched as the target suddenly bounced to her feet and took off down the path. She seemed to have noticed him watching her which made him wonder if this was guilty behavior. He just couldn't tell if it was or if she were just an innocent victim, and his readings were not enough to confirm or deny anything. He'd just have to continue the surveillance.

His phone tap was good – at least she still had, and used, a land line for day-to-day stuff, saving her pay-per-use cell phone for when she wasn't at home. He really needed an excuse to get inside her house for a while and set up some monitoring devices. He had tried to slip in several times, but apparently she had several elderly, nosy, and insomniac neighbors who constantly watched her place for her. Every time he thought he could make it inside, he would notice someone's curtains twitching, day or night. He'd try again tonight, but he needed something sure-fire to get him inside for a while.

Roland shook his head and sighed. He really, really hoped she wasn't the problem. She seemed nice and was easy on the eyes – the kind of girl he'd like to get to know better. He shifted his car into gear and headed off to exchange it for his van. He'd have the van in place by the time she got home, if her run took its usual route.

Janice ran past the old white van that had taken up residence on the corner. She didn't even notice it; her neighborhood had a lot of rental property and cars came and went all the time. If she could have seen into the back of it, she would have been very surprised at the banks of equipment it held.

Janice showered and dressed for work; she had the late shift tonight, which was good. Maybe that blasted squirrel would be done with its evening aerobics workout by the time she got home, and she'd actually be able to get some sleep.

She had a few minutes before she had to leave, so she picked up the phone and dialed the first exterminator in the phone book.

Agent James smiled as he saw the number being dialed pop up on his screen. Acme Exterminators? Perfect. He pressed a few buttons to route the call to himself, let the phone ring three times, and then answered it.

"Acme Exterminators. How may I help you?" Five minutes later, he had an appointment tomorrow morning to rid Janice's attic of a squirrel, and a smug smile was on his face. He slipped into the driver's seat and went off to find the sort of clothes he'd need as an exterminator for Acme. The Agency would supply the proper patches for the uniform, and he'd easily pass for the real thing. He'd better alter his appearance a little, though, in case she had noticed him today and had a good memory for faces.

When the doorbell rang the next morning, Janice was ready and waiting. Not only had the squirrel not finished his run before she got home, she had had even stranger dreams and slept even more poorly than the night before. She was seriously considering renting a motel room for a night or two just to get some rest, and she told the exterminator as much.

The man was nice, and nice-looking, and there was something about him that made her want to trust him on sight.

"A squirrel, eh? Are you sure it's a squirrel and not rats or even bats? Let me have a look around that attic of yours, and I'll see what I need to do." Agent James smiled at Janice reassuringly. The idea that her squirrel might actually be rats or bats (she had visibly shuddered at the thought of bats) had her scurrying to point him and his ladder and equipment bag to the attic access.

Janice followed him to the hall under the attic trapdoor. As he climbed the ladder, she had to smile. The man had a NICE butt. Janice appreciated a nice posterior on a man. Trying to think about the man and not the beasts, she walked into the kitchen. The idea of bats potentially flying around was definitely enough to keep her from following the exterminator to the attic. She shuddered again and poured herself another cup of coffee.

In the attic, James smiled at the way his plan was working, then checked his meter. The readings inside the house were so high that he knew he was in the right place. But was Janice his target, was it the "squirrel," or even something else? These things came in so many forms that you really couldn't ever rule anything completely out. He sighed and beamed his flashlight around the attic space just to make sure that there wasn't actually a real pest infestation here.

But the attic did not appear to hold any squirrels, rats or bats. There was no physical evidence of anything living here that shouldn't be - which was bad, from his point of view. That meant that either Janice was his target or it was going to be one of the nastier creatures he was dealing with. And if it was the nastier thing, then Janice might very well be its dinner.

Roland opened his bag and took out several tiny pieces of equipment, quickly deploying them around the attic. A few tiny holes in the ceiling and others were set up. Finally, he put out some traps so that his work looked legitimate and slipped back through the attic entrance to the main floor.

"Well, I've set up some equipment and traps. Hopefully, the equipment will deter it – it's that electronic high frequency stuff – hey, you don't have a hamster or anything, do you?" James asked ingenuously.

Janice smiled wanly. "No, nothing like that. But if this doesn't work, I may be getting a dog and a cat – a dog to chase off the squirrels and a cat to catch the mice!"

"Oh, your landlord doesn't mind?"

"The place is mine – my grandmother left it to me. She died six months ago."

"Oh, hey, I'm sorry. Listen, why don't I look around the kitchen and make sure you don't have any signs of mice in there, too? You know, your grandma was probably getting old, might have let things go a little….." He paused as Janice stared at him suspiciously. "No charge – I just thought I could give you a little added service today." He grinned at her. And he could have a little more of a look-around to see if he could find the source of the readings he was getting from Janice and the house.

"Okay, then. But Grams was pretty spry right up to the end. Her death was quite a shock, really. I came for dinner one night and she was lying in her bed, dead." Janice sniffed back a few tears. "She was a great old lady – really feisty."

Roland checked the cabinets and corners of the kitchen, the basement and any out-of-the-way corners of the house he could think of. He found nothing. Not that he was looking for rodent leavings – he was looking for other sorts of evidence that would be as obvious to his eyes as evidence of rodents would be to a real exterminator.

He left with the promise to check back in a day or two, handing Janice a business card with his cell phone number on it – specially printed for just this occasion.

Janice smiled as the man left. He had been very nice, she thought as she got ready for work. Maybe she would have to find an excuse to call him sooner rather than later. For the first time, she found herself hoping that the squirrel would be back that night.

The squirrel was back, and Janice slept more poorly than ever. She called the exterminator back the next day, and he promised to visit on the following day. "Give my equipment one more day to work," he told her, thinking that he needed a few more days of readings. What he had gotten so far indicated that at least Janice was neither his target nor in immediate danger. From what she had said about her grandmother, he suspected that the thing had fed on the old woman and overestimated how much feeding it could do before it took her over. It would be more careful with Janice. At least James hoped it would. He needed a little more time to gather evidence and plan how he was going to capture the thing. Some of these creatures could be very hard to grab. At least they had to make those noises that could be mistaken for pests as they pulled themselves out of whatever object they had infiltrated to rest and hide. In this case – as with many – it would probably be in the beams of the ceiling. He would have warning before the thing was completely free and able to attack him.

Janice found herself wide awake at two in the morning. That damned creature was making more noise than usual. Finally, she tossed back the bed covers, turned on the lights and put on some sweats. She hauled a ladder out of the garage and set it up under the attic trapdoor. Moments later, flashlight in hand, she shoved the cover to one side and poked her head up in the attic.

Beaming the flashlight around, Janice surveyed the area. There were traps set, just as there should be. But they were empty. The noises continued, but Janice couldn't see where it could be coming from. She pulled herself the rest of the way into the space and started walking around the attic in the uncomfortable crouch the small space demanded. It seemed like whenever she went towards the source of the sound, it moved and came from somewhere else. Nothing appeared to be moving in the beam from her flashlight. Nothing. Finally, she made it all the way around the space and came back to the trapdoor. She sighed as she sat down, dangling her feet over the edge towards the ladder. The noises suddenly stopped.

And then she felt something on the back of her neck.

Agent James woke up with a start. Loud noises were coming from the headset that had slipped off his head. He jammed it back over his ears just in time to hear Janice's clearly panicked voice saying, "Oh my God, oh my God, I've got ghosts!" Thumps and bumps indicated that she was moving rapidly somewhere in the house. He sighed. Great. Now he would get to play paranormal investigator. At least it gave him a reason to put some of his less ordinary equipment out in the open – stuff he couldn't get away with as an exterminator. He just hoped she would try to call a paranormal group for help so that he could intercept the call.

Janice could only find one number listed for a paranormal investigator. Apparently there wasn't a huge call for that field. Fine. That was fine. She didn't care how many there were, she just needed one. She just hoped the ghost wasn't Grams, because she didn't want it in her house no matter whose ghost it was.

Agent James was waiting for the call. He agreed to show up that evening right after dinner, and then he went to change his appearance and get together his "ghost hunting" equipment.

The man at the door looked vaguely familiar to Janice, but she really couldn't place him. He smiled at her and boosted up an equipment case. "Paranormal Investigations. Jeb Andrews. You're Janice?"

She nodded and invited the man in. She spent the next hour explaining things to him. He seemed especially interested in her grandmother's death. She took him through the whole business of the exterminator and the experience in the attic the night before.

"Well, at least I don't have to rule out rodents," he told her cheerfully, while thinking that he was still dealing with parasitic pests – just not ones that anyone would believe in.

The ladder was still standing in the hallway from the night before, and James was soon boosting himself in to the attic again.

Janice opted to stay downstairs once more – the memory of that touch on her neck was far too fresh. But she did watch and smile as he climbed the ladder. His butt was every bit as nice as the exterminator's. If she had to have all of these strange men in her life, at least they had some nice assets.

James put out more equipment and checked some of the equipment he'd left as an exterminator. Then he went back down into the main part of the house and set up several cameras that filmed in other spectrums plus some equipment that no real paranormal investigator would have ever seen or heard of - equipment special to his agency.

"I'm going to leave this stuff running tonight, look at the results tomorrow, and then maybe stay here the next night," he told Janice. He really wanted to stay tonight, but he knew that the creature would detect him when it began to manifest and then not show up. It wouldn't bother with the equipment, but this sort of creature made a point of preying on people who were alone.

He looked at Janice sitting on her couch, half frightened and half hopeful that he could solve her problem. He could feel himself falling for Janice, and that wasn't good. He didn't know if he'd be able to save her, and he didn't how he'd ever get to know her if he did. This was the whole problem with his job.

He shook Janice's hand and told her he'd see her the next day.

Janice went to bed not long after that. This was her day off, and she was exhausted from the lack of sleep lately. Frankly, she was pretty sure she was tired enough to sleep right through the noises in the attic.

That proved to be the case. It wasn't the noises in the attic that awakened her. It was the sound of her bedroom door creaking slightly as it opened.

Janice didn't usually close the door, but all of the cameras in other parts of the house made her a little concerned for her privacy. Janice stirred restlessly at the first creak. As the creaking continued, she realized what was happening. Frozen with fear, she opened her eyes slightly. There was something glowing in the doorway. Oh God, it was the ghost. She suppressed a moan and closed her eyes again. Maybe if she pretended to be asleep it would go away. She hoped the camera in the hallway was working and caught this thing.

She could feel something in the room with her. Carefully she opened her eyes again, and when she did, she screamed.

The thing standing – or hovering – over her wasn't like any ghost she would have expected. No black shadow, no mist, no semi-transparent human form. It was glowing blue-white, true, but it looked like a gauze curtain being moved by the wind. Some of the gauzy stuff was beginning to form tentacles.

Several of the tentacles reached towards her and she screamed again. Somewhere in the back of her mind, she thought she heard the front door burst open, but all she could think of were those tentacles reaching, reaching, sliding into her ears...

A blinding light seared her eyes, and in the afterimages she thought she saw the guy who had been watching her from the car the other day, and then the room, and the world, went black.

Janice stretched and rolled over in bed. She felt so completely rested this morning – it was really nice. That trap she got from the humane society must have caught the squirrel since it hadn't kept her awake half the night.

She had some memory of a strange dream, but even as she thought about it, the last remnants of it faded away.

As she ate breakfast, Janice remembered a few dregs of the dream – it seemed to include an exterminator and a paranormal investigator, both with nice posteriors, but she wasn't sure. Finally, she put her ladder up to the attic opening and poked her head up there to take a look around. The space was actually abnormally clean, as if someone had been up there and cleared out the dust, and the trap was actually empty. Janice left it there. The squirrel seemed to have left, but she'd leave the trap in place for a few more days, just in case.

There was something strange about the attic, or there had been – but that must just have been her dream. She shrugged and climbed back down the ladder.

That afternoon the doorbell rang. It was a nice-looking young man with a small computer who said he was doing a survey for his college class. "I'm not using phones because I like to look at people when I ask them questions. Besides, it's harder to slam the door on me than it is to hang up the phone," he said, smiling at her winningly.

She stood on the porch with him to answer his questions, mostly about her political affiliations. He seemed a bit familiar, but then all the men she met lately seemed that way. Maybe it was a sign that she needed to start dating again.

As the young man walked away, she watched his butt – it seemed awfully familiar, somehow.

Agent Roland James sighed as he walked away. Janice seemed perfectly normal. It seemed that his memory adjustment had worked and Janice was suffering from no ill effects from her experiences. In a few days, her energy levels should return to normal, and she was no longer in danger of being taken over. His work here was ended, and he would not be seeing Janice again. Sometimes, once the lives were saved, his job really did suck.

IT'S CELLAR TIME

Gladys Dixon sighed and put her teacup down with a little more force than necessary when the doorbell rang. Her terrier-mixed-with-something-large-and-hairy dog, Frankie, barked ferociously and raced for the door. Gladys scolded him as she made her way to the door, but when she looked through the peephole to see who was there, she decided that Frankie hadn't barked nearly ferociously enough. Really, she thought, it was a pity that he was actually quite gentle. She'd love to see him take a chunk out of the seat of the pants of the nuisance on the other side of the door.

Gritting her teeth and trying to turn it into a gracious smile, Gladys opened the door to the man waiting there, thinking that she'd never seen an oilier-looking man in all of her long life - not even the snake-oil salesmen of her youth.

Jonathan Tucker smoothed down his hair and plastered a toothy grin on his face as the door opened. Good – it was just the old lady. That great-nephew of hers wasn't here today, just like he'd hoped. Maybe the old lady would be a little more receptive of his offer when she was alone. And old people were so easy to gull, he thought. Just some money, an offer of a reduced rate in one of his full-service retirement communities, and they were falling all over themselves to let him take their old monsters of houses off their hands. They didn't need to know that he was offering them rock-bottom prices and would make a killing on the developments he put on their land once he tore down their old eyesores. And they certainly didn't need to know that the reduced rates in his retirement villages were still anything but cheap. He thought about the grounds this Victorian heap was set on and smiled even bigger at the thought of the lot the size of an entire block.

"Mrs. Dixon, good afternoon!" he smiled at her. "You're looking lovely this afternoon. Wonderful weather we're having, isn't it?"

Gladys Dixon successfully hid her wince and stepped outside the door onto the large old-fashioned porch that wound all the way around the house. She had no intention of letting that man inside her home. "Mr. Tucker, how are you today?"

"Well, Mrs. Dixon, that all depends." He stopped expectantly.

"Depends?" Gladys knew full well what it depended on, but she was not going to give the man an inch.

"Why, yes, Mrs. Dixon. Don't you remember? We were discussing how much I was going to pay you to take this place off your hands before you have to put any more money into repairs. You were thinking about the price." He spoke gently, as if she were having trouble understanding him.

So he was going to play it that way, was he? Gladys snapped the door shut behind her and stepped towards Jonathan before she spoke. "I remember quite well that I told you that I have no intention of selling my home to you now or at any point in the future, Mr. Tucker. I am not senile, and I know I was not thinking about a price. Now please leave." Her gimlet eyes drilled holes in him, and the dog by her feet growled, showing its teeth.

Jonathan looked at the dog and backed up. "You might want to control your dog," he said. "The city doesn't look kindly on aggressive dogs." Then his voice went back to oily.

"You really should sell to me, you know. You'll come out ahead in the long run. A nice place to live with people looking after you, a few dollars in the bank for that nephew of yours to inherit, and no more worries about this heap and the bills it generates. Why, the heat in the winter and the water for the lawn in the summer must be phenomenal," he said as he stumbled backward down the front steps. He nearly fell, and Gladys had to bite her lip to keep from smiling.

She stepped forward, following him. Thinking she was following him out of interest, he kept going. "Our Sunset Village is perfect for an active, able-bodied woman like you. Seniors only, so there aren't any noisy young people like you have in this neighborhood, and you won't have any lawn to worry about, or maintenance, and there's bingo and shuffleboard and cards and …."

Mrs. Dixon had been following him step for step as he backed down the flagstone walk. Now she lost her battle with herself, abandoning the good manners and graciousness that had been ingrained in her from the time she could walk.

"Mr. Tucker," she snapped. "Allow me to put this in terms even one so self-centered and stupid as you can understand. I will not sell to you now or ever. You will never get your hands on this place, not even over my dead body. Never!" With that, she backed him out of the gate and slammed and locked the wrought-iron confection behind him. It was head-high, and the fence it went with was the same height with points – sharp ones – on top of it. Without another word, she turned and marched back up the walk. She stalked into the house and slammed the front door behind her, throwing the bolt home for good measure. Then she leaned against the door and stood there, Frankie panting at her feet. "Frankie," she said, "why do I get a feeling that that man is trouble?"

The grandfather clock on the landing struck four, and she sighed again. "Cellar time," she said to Frankie. It was time for her daily duties in the basement, and they wouldn't wait while she finished her tea. Gladys was not one who shirked her duties, particularly this one. Leaving Frankie behind to bark through the window at the retreating Tucker, she shut herself into the basement staircase and descended the steps to the old, stone cellar.

Jonathan Tucker was not happy. How dared she! That old harpy was going to sell to Tuckertown Enterprises, he had no doubt in his mind. And he was done playing nice. The gloves were coming off; this was war. Not even over her dead body, eh? Well, he hoped it wouldn't come to that.

With the barks of Frankie still echoing behind him, he straightened his suit jacket and stormed off down the block. He had a good idea of just what would make a good impetus for the old woman to move. He'd used this trick before, and it invariably worked quite well. But first, he needed Frankie to be somewhere else. A trip to the vet would be just the ticket. Jonathan hurried home to find the things he needed.

"George, that horrible Tucker man was here again," Gladys was saying into the phone, talking to her grand-nephew. "Yes, he was just as insistent as ever. I'm afraid I lost my temper with him, but you know as well as I do that I can't let this place go. Not now and maybe not ever." Frankie whined to go out, pawing at the back door. Absently, she opened it and let him out into the huge yard. She sighed. "Not that I'd really want to sell it, anyway. You know it goes to you, don't you? Yes, I know you love it as much as I do. You know, you really should just move in here with me…" She laughed before he could answer. "However, I'm afraid living with an old lady would cramp your style. But seriously, you need to learn more about the care and feeding…" Frankie barked at the door, wanting back in. "All right, I'll see you tomorrow, dear. Have a good evening."

Gladys looked down at Frankie and said, "Want a treat?" but stopped with her hand half-way to the treat jar. Frankie had something all over his hairy muzzle. It was wet, and when she leaned over to get a better look, she smelled something sweet, and something she had read last week jumped into her head. "Anti-freeze! Oh, I hope not...Frankie, where did you get into that?!"

Grabbing his leash, Gladys dragged the bewildered dog out to her elderly car and rumbled off for the emergency vet's office in the next town.

Jonathan Tucker watched as the beautifully maintained 1950's Ford Fairlane barreled by and smiled. That had worked out even better than he hoped. He was thinking that she would be taking a sick dog to the vet later tonight or tomorrow, but if she left now, so much the better.

Under the cover of darkness, he slipped through the driveway gate that Gladys, in her haste, had left open and through the lilac bushes up to the house. Out of curiosity, he tried the back door, but it was locked. No loss. He put on his gloves and pulled a small set of tools out of his pocket. He was inside in a few minutes.

Taking a few moments to look around, he could see why Mrs. Dixon wasn't taking his usual bait about home repairs. Like the outside, the inside was in incredibly good condition. The place was still an elegant Victorian showplace, and even Jonathan Tucker, who wouldn't let anything older than this year's style through his front door, had to admit the place was beautiful. But sentimentality had no place in his personality, and he didn't allow himself to be distracted for long. He quickly located the cellar door.

The cellar door was also locked, and Jonathan grumbled as he took his picks out of his pocket again. Who locked their cellar door? And this wasn't a typical cellar door. This thing looked like something from the Middle Ages that was made to hold off the invading hordes – big, solid planks that were set with huge metal hinges. The lock on it was better than the one on the back door. Was Mrs. Dixon afraid of something coming up from the cellar? Did she think it was haunted or something? At that thought, Jonathan looked around uneasily and then shone a flashlight down the cellar stairs. But he didn't hear anything and nothing appeared to be amiss, so he shrugged at his fantasies and headed down the stairs.

Except for the fact that the place was made of stone like some sort of dungeon, it was actually quite dry and warm down in the basement. The main room was huge, with quite a few doors opening off of it. Through one open door, Jonathan could see an ancient furnace sprawling out like some sort of monster. He took note of where it was and then found what he was looking for – a window to the back of the house in a dark corner of the room.

The window was a large one; in a modern home, it would be called an egress window and Jonathan was surprised to see it in such an old house. It was also the only one he could see that was not completely barred over. This place was a dungeon indeed. This window was of the old-fashioned double hung sort, but it slid up wide enough to climb out to a small space and ladder.

Peering out, Tucker could see that it exited behind one of the lilacs that grew so abundantly on the property.

This was perfect. Humming to himself happily, Jonathan opened the window and then worked with it until it would slide up and down smoothly.

Finally, he looked around for any drains that might be in the floor. He found one and, prying the opening up, stuffed it full of leaves and sticks and other debris from the window well. He fastened the grate down again and then left the house as silently as he had come in. He made a point of unlocking several gates on the property before he left.

Several hours later, around midnight, Jonathan returned. He paused briefly near the fire hydrant on Gladys's block. Since hers was the only house on the block, and the rest of the area was dedicated to big lots and huge old trees, there weren't any people around to see what he was doing. He quickly pulled a large roll of fire hose from the back of his van and stashed it behind a bush by Gladys's wrought iron fence. Then he parked several blocks away and scurried back in the moonless night.

It was the work of moments to connect the hose to the hydrant. Then he ran it through the fence and over to the window he had opened earlier. A quick check of the garage revealed the old woman's car. She was back and the lack of lights indicated that she was asleep. Carefully, he threaded the hose through the window and let it down to the floor. A shelf on the wall nearby kept the hose from the view of the staircase. Finally, Jonathan returned to the hydrant and turned it on. The hose plumped up satisfyingly, and Jonathan took himself to a handy hiding spot for the next few hours.

An hour or so before dawn, he returned and reversed the process. The hose was heavier and harder to deal with, but Jonathan had practiced this maneuver before and quickly had it stowed in the back of his van. No one had come along to see anything, and when Mrs. Dixon got up, she would be very surprised at the state of her basement. He hadn't actually looked; shining a light into an occupied house was not his idea of safe vandalism, but the water had run for a very long time.

Jonathan Tucker took himself home to his soft bed and expensive sheets as a pleasant reward for a job well done.

One look into the basement that morning had Gladys Dixon in a panic. She was on the phone to her nephew George immediately, and Jonathan Tucker would have been gratified by the way the young man's car came screaming up to the house.

"George, I don't know what to think, and I'm afraid to go down there alone," said Mrs. Dixon.

"Of all the things to happen – a flood! Fortunately only one of the drains appears to be jammed, so it's not as bad as it could be, but you know the possible results as well as I do! After all the work we've done to keep it warm and dry down there, for this to happen….I just don't understand. It must have been ground water, and the sump pumps must have failed." She gulped and then squared her shoulders. "Well, now that you're here, let's go downstairs and take a look at the damages."

Followed by George, who was a big, brawny fellow whose size alone inspired courage, Gladys carefully descended the cellar stairs.

Jonathan Tucker would have been surprised at what awaited her. Despite the amount of water he had pumped into the basement, there was only a small pool left by the jammed drain. The rest of the area was damp, but only barely.

The two carefully approached the door next to the furnace room. If Jonathan had looked around a bit more when he was down there, he would have noted with surprise that this door was even heavier and more carefully locked than the one at the top of the stairs. Now, however, a small trickle of water was running under the door – uphill into the room - from the puddle by the drain.

Mrs. Dixon kicked at it irritably. "Greedy thing," she said. "George, grab the mop and put an end to this little sippy-straw, would you?" George did so quickly. He was not excited about seeing what was on the other side of the door.

"Auntie, why don't we just leave it be? I mean, we can't really do anything about it, and it might be dangerous…"

"It's pathetic to see a big, strong man like you whine, George, so don't," Gladys snapped.

George winced.

"And it's not 'might be dangerous'; the thing is dangerous. It's dangerous at the best of times, and right now it could be downright deadly. But we need to see exactly how bad it is. If nothing else, I can fire up the furnace and try to dry it out a little bit." She sighed. "If Grandfather had ANY idea what he was doing…of course if he had had any idea, he wouldn't have been a bumbling fool and we wouldn't be stuck with this thing." She turned to George, who had decided that he could not let a 70-year-old woman show him up.

"Let's go then, Auntie, and get this over with." He put out his hand for the key ring and soon had the door unlocked. Carefully they eased it open and peered inside.

It was pitch dark in the room, as there were no windows. Since they were blocking the light from the door, George turned on a flashlight and aimed it around the room. All too soon, the beam came to rest on what could only be described as an upright puddle. It had originally been in a corner of the room but now it seemed to be squeezing up against an invisible barrier near the middle of the room, and it looked as though it might burst out at any moment.

"Still contained, then, despite all of the water. Good." Gladys's relief was palpable.

"And you won't have to feed it for weeks, maybe months," added George. "Why do we feed it, anyway? Won't it just dry up if we don't give it more water?"

"No," Gladys shook her head. "Father tried that. It made a terrible noise and started shaking the entire house. We still don't know how or why. We just know that the one time it got out of the containment circle, it tried to eat us, and if we don't feed it water, it makes hellish noises and shakes the house. Finding a balance of feeding it took decades, Father said, and we don't want to upset it." Gladys was locking the door back up as she spoke.

"Father used to say that some families have skeletons in their closets. We have a water elemental in ours. Or something like that. We've never really been sure what it was that Grandfather summoned, since he didn't survive the encounter. If we could get rid of it, we would. But we can't, and you'll inherit the family curse when I die."

George laughed and said, "Auntie, you keep giving me reasons to wish you a VERY long life! If that Tucker fellow had any idea what he'd be getting into if he ever managed to buy this house…" George laughed the whole way up the stairs.

Jonathan Tucker woke late and stretched luxuriously. He wouldn't bother Mrs. Dixon today - that might seem suspicious - but he would drive by and see if he could see repair vehicles and pumping units at her house. The thought made him smile. Just a few more days and he'd have his hands on a block large enough to put multiple luxury condominium units on and then he'd mop up. Again. The play on words made him chuckle. Flooded basements and mopping up financially. He was a clever man, wasn't he?

Later that morning, Jonathan Tucker sat in his fancy sports car and fumed. There were no plumber and no trucks bearing pumps at the Victorian mansion. Mrs. Dixon and her nephew were outside, in fact, directing some workers from a landscaping firm as they cleared an area for play equipment for the smallest of the nieces and nephews. He slipped out of his car and crept closer to the fence to listen. Maybe they'd talk about the basement.

"The sandbox needs to go over there, and the fort and climber over here. No, young man, you do NOT need to take down that lilac. Lilacs were made for children to play under."

Nearby George was indicating where the cedar mulch was to be spread. "Wish we'd had this when I was little, Auntie!" he called over to her. "Although the tire swing and the tree house were good. You aren't getting rid of them, are you?"

"Of course not. Children need tire swings and tree houses as well as these new, fancier things. Don't worry, I won't tread on your memories, George!" She chuckled. "I like to bring the best of the old and new together here. And the little ones will be here on Sunday to try it all out." She paused, smiling. "The vet said that Frankie should be ready to join them by then. I'm so glad - he does love playing with the children and they with him." She paused. "I still want to know where he got into the anti-freeze. I think I found a trace where the fence is close to the road; I suppose someone might have had a leaky radiator and parked there for a while. The vet said it was a very good thing I got him there so quickly, though. They got most of it out of him before it had a chance to do much damage. That reminds me. George, could you come with me to pick him up on Friday?"

Jonathan pricked up his ears at this. A family gathering. If he could do some more damage by then, surely the family would gang up on her and force her to move someplace safer. Families tended to think that old people living by themselves were just asking for trouble, and he could arrange to have that pointed out. And that dog was still alive. Well, he hadn't really set out to kill it, just take it out of the picture for a bit.

Even though he listened for quite a while, they never referred to the basement, and he slunk away, thinking that maybe they just hadn't seen the damage. Meanwhile, what step did he want to take next? He hummed as he got back into his car. It was a pity that he'd have to tear out that little playground when he started construction. Maybe he'd save the equipment and put it up in another spot. Even though his condos were adults-only, he sometimes added a small picnic area with play equipment for visitors. It was good for sales.

The next day still showed no signs of pumps or plumbers, and Jonathan decided that maybe there must have been more drains that he had missed and the water pressure had been lower than he had thought. Well, he knew the old lady would be leaving to pick up the dog on Friday, and the nephew would be with her. The landscaping people should be done by then, so Friday would be the best time for his next move.

On Friday, when Gladys got into George's SUV for the trip to the vet's, Jonathan was ready. He slipped through the bushes and straight to the window he had left unlocked. He was quickly in the cellar in the furnace room.

The furnace was an antique monster. Originally coal, it had been converted to run on gas. It was so old and big that no one would be surprised when it malfunctioned and started a fire. Good thing for him it was still chilly enough at night for the furnace to be on occasionally.

It struck him how efficient the thing must be. Odd, for something so big and old. The cellar was exceedingly warm and dry. Well, it was going to be a lot warmer and drier in a little bit.

He located some rags and newspapers – cellars always seemed to have those, and Mrs. Dixon's did not disappoint. He put them near the furnace, did a few things to it, opened the door to the pilot light, and made it look like someone forgot to close up the furnace properly. He ran a small wick from the pilot to the rags and papers. Then he beat a hasty retreat to the upstairs where he turned up the thermostat.

He was at his favorite sports bar watching the game a few minutes later – with lots of witnesses. When Gladys and George brought Frankie home from the vet, nothing seemed to be amiss. But when they stepped inside, the smell of something burning hit them like a slap in the face.

George put Frankie down on the porch and shoved Gladys outside. "Wait here!" he shouted. With what was in the basement, neither one of them wanted to have to call the fire department.

He grabbed a fire extinguisher from the kitchen and followed the smoke smell to the basement stairs. The door was cool, and there wasn't any smoke coming out from under the door. In fact, here, the smell was a wet-burnt smell.

Gladys had followed him, and when she smelled the wet odor, she quickly opened up the basement door and followed George down the stairs.

At the bottom, she stopped, mouth open.

George had stopped short. "What the…"

"It appears that our over-fed friend has done us a good deed, George." Gladys pushed open the charred, soaking wet door to the normally locked room. The door to the furnace room was partially burnt off, and the rafters were sooty in that room. There was a door in between the two rooms and it was completely burnt away. The floor was wet in both rooms, and in the water elemental's room, the creature itself was a shrunken memory of what it had looked like several days before. It was trembling and making a small keening noise.

"I didn't know it could do that," remarked George. "Especially since it can't leave the circle."

"Neither did I, but clearly it can. I guess it never had a reason to do it before. But it must have shot that water all over the place when it felt threatened by fire," Gladys said. "I never thought I'd feel grateful to that monster, but right now I certainly do."

She fetched a bucket of water from a sink on the other side of the basement and dumped it in a trough that fed into the circle. The thing in there soaked it up, plumped up a bit and stopped making noises. She gave it another one for good measure.

"I see what you mean, Auntie, about when it needs to be fed. But it really was a lucky thing that the basement flooded the other day, isn't it?" He was spraying the fire extinguisher up at the beams, but they were literally dripping and any fires were completely out.

"Leave it. There's nothing but a cement slab for the garage over the furnace room. It's warm and I don't really need the furnace on right now. Let's turn off the gas, and I'll see if some of the cousins will look at it on Sunday."

They went back up the stairs and locked the door to the cellar. Frankie had wandered inside and was staring hopefully at the treat jar. He had never had the promised treat several nights ago and clearly thought that he should have it now. Gladys laughed and gave him several, happy to have him home again. She sent George to the store for chicken and potatoes for mountains of fried chicken and potato salad so she could start to cook for Sunday, and life seemed to go back to normal.

Jonathan was shocked when no fire trucks screamed past the bar on the way to Mrs. Dixon's house. Later that evening he carefully cruised past. George was out in the yard putting up a shelter for Sunday's family get-together and he could see Gladys on the porch with her dog at her feet. He could swear that the dog saw him and he sped away before anyone else could notice him.

The next day the family gathered. The children loved the new play equipment, everyone brought something to go with the fried chicken and potato salad, and a small contingent of men repaired the doors in the basement. They all remarked on the good fortune of the earlier flood. One of the men worked for a heating company and checked out the furnace. Puzzled, he declared it in good working order.

"You didn't leave the furnace door open, did you?" he asked. "You can't do that with this kind. And since when do you store old paper and other flammables in here?"

"No, of course not. I haven't touched anything but the thermostat for weeks. And I store the papers on the far side of the basement, usually. I don't understand."

"Neither do I," said the cousin. "But what with that and the flood, I think I'll be coming around a bit more often for a while. Our friend in there," and he nodded to the monster's room, "might be gaining a few talents. Or maybe he has another friend hanging around."

George added, "And Auntie has been asking me to move in. I'll go ahead and do it this week."

No one noticed the unlocked window, and no one suspected a human element.

Jonathan spent the week seething. His plans were not working, and he really wanted to get that property purchased and demolition started as soon as possible. He had a timeline that he intended to stick to. His last project was ending, and this one needed to begin.

He let another week go by and then stopped by the house again when he saw George in the yard. That George had moved in had not escaped his notice, and he thought that perhaps he could talk the young man into getting Gladys to sell. After all, why on earth would a young man like George want to devote his youth to looking after an old lady and an even older house when he could be having fun?

George saw the man coming. The guy was even oilier-looking than Auntie had described. Nasty fellow, George decided, and their conversation just reinforced that notion. Tucker spent the whole time trying to talk George into getting Gladys to sell. George was highly insulted. Even if Auntie didn't need him, he'd still enjoy living with her. She was lively and alert and great to talk to. He was having a great deal of fun teaching her about his favorite bands, and they shared a love of science fiction, with many of the same favorite authors. He still went out with his buddies, and if he wanted to have anyone over, well, the house was more than big enough.

He let Jonathan go on for quite a while before he finally got fed up and said, "Are you done? Because I am. Let me show you to the gate." And grabbing the man by the collar, he escorted him to the gate, put him through it, and locked it behind him much as Gladys had done several weeks before. Then he stalked off to the house to complain to his aunt about the extra-large pest that had suddenly appeared in the garden and had needed removal.

To say that Jonathan was furious was an understatement. His rage was without boundaries. Not only was the old lady a stubborn old biddy, but her great-nephew was a stupid, hulking road block. Probably thought he'd get a better inheritance if she didn't sell out. That was it – all holds were off. Tonight he'd come back to the house, dog or not, and finish the problem. Any other inheritors would probably be happy to get the property off their hands after tonight.

Jonathan waited until all of the lights were out, and then waited a little longer. Then he slipped into the yard, climbed down into the window well and through the window into the cellar. He had a small penlight on him, but didn't want to risk a larger flashlight just in case. He shone the light around the room. He needed the furnace room again, but he thought he remembered where it was. This time he was going to open the gas. A little while for buildup, a match through the window, and boom. Problem solved. And there wouldn't even be a need for much demolition.

He went up to the door and snarled. Locked. Who locked furnace rooms? He pulled out his picks and within minutes had the door open. He dropped his penlight and it broke on the stone floor. No matter. He knew where the furnace was, and he could always turn on the light for just a minute or two. There weren't any windows in the room that he recalled. He was feeling his way along the wall, looking for a light switch when it occurred to him that he was in the wrong room; the furnace room wall wasn't this long.

A huge boom shook the house, waking up Gladys and George. Frankie ran in circles, barking, and they all raced for the cellar door, the source of the noise.

George felt the cellar door. It was cool. They sniffed – there was a slight smell of ozone, but nothing else. Carefully he unlocked the door, and they crept down the stairs. Gladys turned on the light. The door to the monster's room was open, but the place was utterly still. She peered into the room and then turned on the light. The room was empty. The circle was still on the floor in the corner, but there was nothing in it. For the first time in nearly a century, the room was unoccupied. There was a charred place in the middle of the circle that had not been there before, but no water, no puddle, and no monster.

George gasped. "It escaped!"

"No, no, I don't believe it did. I think it's gone. I don't know how or why, but I know I don't feel its presence for the first time in my life," Gladys said carefully.

"But how? You told me that with all of the research your father did, the only thing he thought that would get rid of it was for someone to cross into the circle."

"Yes, and he was going to do that himself when he was ready to go, but then he was lost in that airplane crash, and couldn't. I was going to try when my time came, you know."

"I didn't," George replied with a scowl. "But that doesn't explain what happened here."

Frankie had followed them down to the basement. He had found the open window and was sniffing and trying to climb through the window well. George noticed, and he and Gladys went over to have a look.

"I think we may have had a burglar," she said thoughtfully. "Do you think we should call the police?"

George shrugged. "Sure, why not. It's not like we have anything to hide." His eyes drifted back to the now-empty room.

The police came; of course there was nothing for them to see, but the break-in was duly reported.

Later that week, Gladys read in the paper that the abandoned vehicle of real estate developer Jonathan Tucker had been found, but the man himself was missing. The article intimated that Tucker was known for shady dealing and had perhaps "disappeared," either with or without help.

She showed the article to George. "I wonder," she said.

George raised his eyebrows. "Well, if it was him, he did us a favor. You can go on that trip and I don't have to worry about trying to find a wife who understands that I have a monster in my basement!"

Jane W. Wolfinbarger

JUST LIKE CLOCKWORK

Bits and pieces of clockwork. They were scattered everywhere in the house. Every time Josiah Banks could, he visited junk shops, antique shops, flea markets - anywhere he might find an old, wind-up style alarm clock or watch. He had tried the newer ones, but too often nowadays the gears inside were made of plastic. "And I need metal gears, metal ones!" he would mutter to himself as he rummaged through a box of miscellaneous junk at a yard sale or auction.

Each clock or watch was taken home and carefully disassembled, and the gears, large and small, were sorted according to size in piles that had started in his workroom and eventually overflowed into his living room. But that was all right, because no one ever came to visit him anymore, not since the time he got upset with his favorite aunt and uncle for accidently mixing up two piles of gears.

These days he was invited other places and happily went visiting, because Josiah was sociable, just very intense about his clockwork.

"Josiah," his friend Andy would say, as he carefully placed a glass of soda between two piles of tiny gears on the coffee table, careful not to knock over either one, "Josiah, what are you going to do with all these gears?" Andy was the only friend left who was brave enough to come and see Josiah as his house.

"Build something, of course," Josiah replied seriously.

"But you've been collecting the dratted things for years! You must have enough to build something by now?"

"Maybe. I'll know when I have enough," Josiah said, shrugging. He wasn't about to admit to Andy that he had actually built something already. His workroom was in his basement where no one else ever went. He was careful to keep the blinds pulled and the door shut, so no one could see what he was doing down there. He passed Andy a plate of homemade chocolate chip cookies that his Aunt Agnes had sent him, and that was the end of the subject.

When Andy left later on that day, Josiah looked around the room at the piles of clockwork, really noticing for the first time what it must look like to an outsider. The piles were all over the room, falling over untidily, dusty and, in some cases, rusty, and covering almost every flat surface. There were thousands of the things. "Almost. I'm almost ready," he said to himself. "I just need that one big set..."

That weekend he found what he was looking for. A massive grandfather clock, whose once-elegant case had been ruined in a flood, was waiting for him at an auction with other flood-damaged goods. Josiah gasped when he saw it, and counted the money he had with him three times over to see how high he could bid on it. In the end, it went home with him, along with a few smaller alarm clocks for good measure.

He worked far into the night, carefully taking the clock apart and examining the gears and mainspring. They were in perfect condition, and he carefully placed them on his living room sofa in a place of honor.

On Monday, he arranged to take a week off work. He took care of all his bills, the shopping, the laundry, and anything that could distract him, took the phone off the hook, canceled dinner with Aunt Agnes and Uncle Ben, and told Andy that he wouldn't be available for a while. Then he locked the door, rubbed his hands together, and descended to his basement.

His pet rat, Clicker, came scurrying up to him as he turned on the light. He picked up Clicker absently and put him on his shoulder, staring around the room as he did. Everything down here was in place and seemed to be holding its breath in anticipation. Josiah went over to where the pieces of sheet metal he had cut, shaped and welded were ready and waiting for him. Then he gave a great, wobbling sigh, and reached for the first piece. He had been waiting for this moment for so long...

The week was busy. Josiah ran up and down the stairs, retrieving gears of various sizes and spent long hours with a magnifying lens strapped over his eyes. Clicker scuttled over the bench keeping him company as the days wore into nights and back into days again. Several times, Josiah woke up to find that he had fallen asleep at his workbench and had several sizes of gear imprinted on his cheek.

By the end of the week, he was working at a feverish pace, no longer stopping even to eat. The piles of gears upstairs were disappearing and the newest, biggest gears had long since been fitted into place. The shaped pieces of metal had been welded together and finally, Josiah was almost done. As he held the last piece of clockwork in his hands, he looked at it with tears in his eyes. Then he smiled and carefully put the piece in place.

The next day, Andy came knocking at the front door. The week was up and he was determined to know what Josiah had been up too all this time. When Josiah didn't answer, he peered in the front windows. To his surprise, the living room was clean. No, it was beyond clean. It was immaculate. Startled, he returned to the door and knocked louder. Just as he was ready to give up, he heard a noise from inside like the slamming of a door and then the lock on the front door clicked open.

Josiah opened the door and stood there, looking at Andy. He was gaunt, and there were huge circles under his eyes, but he looked happy - happier than Andy had seen him look in ages, in fact. He grinned hugely when he saw Andy, and said, "Come in! I was just about to call you! I'm done! It's finished. After all these years, it's done!" He stepped aside and motioned Josiah into the spotless front room.

"What's done? And where are all the gears...Oh, wait a minute, you mean you finally used those things and made something?" Andy stood staring around the room, looking to see what Josiah had made.

"Yes I did! I've worked all week, and it's finally done!" Josiah crowed.

"Great! When can I see it? Is it up here?" Andy asked, pushing into the room. The movement of something scuttling under the sofa caught his eye. "What was that? A rat!?" he exclaimed as he realized what he had seen.

"Oh, that's just Clicker. He's my pet. I usually keep him downstairs, but now, well, I really don't need to." Josiah knelt on the floor and pulled Clicker out from under the sofa.

Andy got a good look at Clicker and his mouth fell open. "Josiah, is this what you made? A clockwork rat? He's amazing!" He reached for the rat, who was indeed made of clockwork.

Josiah handed Clicker over to Andy and smiled hugely. Clicker was amazing, he had no doubt of that. "Do you like him?"

Andy examined the clockwork rat. "Josiah, this is more than amazing. I mean, I can see that this is made of clockwork and you wind him up, but he is acting like a real rat. Just the mechanics of him are astounding - he has joints that act like real ones - but, Josiah, he's acting like a real pet rat!"

"I know. He came out pretty well. But he was just my first project. I made him quite a while ago." Josiah was still grinning like mad. "I've done a lot more since then."

"You mean that you have even bigger and better stuff than this?" Andy looked back up at his friend.

"Yep, sure do! And I'll show you in just a few minutes - I was waiting for you to be here for the grand unveiling!" Josiah said with pride.

"What else have you made?" asked Andy, handing the rat back to Josiah.

"Oh, I made clockwork dog, and a few others small animals, but I ended up taking them apart again so that I could re-use the gears and the brain material."

"Brain material?" Andy got a funny look on his face.

Josiah laughed, saying, "Not real brains, Andy. Just some stuff in a bag that I found with a set of gears one time at an auction. You know I've always loved clockwork, ever since I was a little kid, and I've haunted auctions for the stuff for years. A couple of years ago, I bid on a big lot of loose gears, some plans, and what they called miscellaneous junk in a box. When I got it home I found that the miscellaneous junk and plans included a bag of sand-like stuff and some notes."

"Go on," Andy encouraged when Josiah paused.

"Well, the notes were by someone who had been trying to make a clockwork man. The intact plans were for a rat and a dog and a cat - there was one page of stuff about a man, but it was pretty torn up. The person who wrote the notes created this, this, brain-stuff, it's sort of like sand - I guess it must be silicone or something. I really don't know how it works. I just know that it does." Josiah confessed. "That's what's inside Clicker."

"So you decided to make a clockwork man."

"Yes, and he's done. Since the plans weren't complete, I had to figure out part of him myself. And I used up all the brain-sand on him, so I can't make another one like him. But Andy, he's going to be amazing! Come on down and we'll wind him up!" said Josiah.

Andy was examining Clicker again as they descended into the basement. "How are you going to get him to do things?" he asked. He looked around at the big open room which he had never seen before. It was pretty empty. There was a few bit of clockwork here and there on a very tidy workbench along one wall. A few more tools were on the metal shelves attached to the opposite wall. Like the upstairs, the room was immaculate.

"Well, I suppose he'll have to learn. Clicker here was a bit wild at first, really afraid of me...but he tamed down pretty quickly." Josiah walked over to a sheet draped something roughly man-sized in the middle of the room. He whisked it off, and there stood his clockwork man.

"Wow. Just wow!" said Andy, his eyes sparkling. "This is really neat, Josiah." And the man was. He had a round head and body and articulated joints. Josiah had even put a pleasant expression on the man's welded face. A large key stuck out of the middle of the man's back.

"So what took you so long to make him?" Andy asked as Josiah prepared to wind the man up for the first time.

"I needed to find a certain type of clock for parts and I had a hard time finding it. Last weekend, I got it." Josiah finished winding the man and then paused with his finger on a switch. He cleared his throat importantly. "LADIES AND GENTLEMEN!" he proclaimed theatrically, "I GIVE TO YOU THE ONE AND ONLY, THE FIRST, THE AMAZING, CLOCKWORK MAN!!!"

And he flipped the switch.

There was a whirring, and a little clicking sound as the gears began to move inside. The man's arms moved, and he turned his head back and forth. Then his legs moved, and he moved forward and backwards. His head turned towards Josiah and Andy.

And then all hell broke loose.

The clockwork man ran from Josiah and Andy, clearly terrified. He rammed into the workbench, scattering leftover gears everywhere. Then he charged towards the stairs. He got up to the fourth stair before the weight of his metal body broke through the treads and sent him tumbling back down again. Undeterred, the clockwork man still tried to get away. This time he managed to crash into the post holding up the rest of the stairs and the entire staircase collapsed.

Josiah and Andy had stared in shock as the clockwork man began his frantic attempt at escape. By the time he broke the bottom steps, they had fled to the far side of the room, and as the whole staircase came down, they climbed to the top of the metal shelving units and crouched there, watching in shock as the man destroyed the rest of the workbench, running into it and trying to climb on top of it.

Josiah whispered to Andy, "These are anchored to the wall with big bolts. I think we'll be safe here."

Andy looked back at him, his eyes huge with fear. "A little wild, you said. Maybe take a while to tame down? My God, man, this thing is dangerous! You said that plans you found, they were torn up? How badly torn up were they?"

Josiah swallowed then blanched. "I didn't think about it before, but they were pretty torn up. And there were some stains...I thought someone had spilled cocoa on them..."

"Cocoa. Right. Try bloodstains. Old, torn up plans with bloodstains on them for something no one ever heard of before. Brains-in-a-bag. Not such a good idea, maybe?" Andy sniped.

"Yeah, maybe. I didn't really think. I just wanted to make him - it was like a dream come true for me." He shuddered. "Now it's a nightmare." He looked around the room. "I wonder if we could reach the window from the edge of this shelf without falling." He eyed the distance speculatively.

Andy looked at it and shook his head. "I don't think so. And I'd hate to think what would happen if we fell and he ran into us. We'll just have stay up here until he winds down. At least we have a chance to get away."

They watched as Clicker scuttled across the floor and the man tried to get away from Clicker, ramming into the shelf next to them. It held tight to the wall, but they could still feel the impact. Tools flew everywhere.

"Uh, yeah, about that. The reason it took me so long to be able to make him?" Josiah swallowed again, and closed his eyes.

"Go on..."

"Well, I was waiting for a special sort of clock, with a special sort of winding mechanism. The one I found this past weekend." He paused again.

"And?"

Another crash sounded below them, and the shelving unit shook again.

"Well, it was called a Seven Day Wonder, the sort of clock you only wind once a week."

BEHIND THE GATE

Alex edged closer to the rusty wrought-iron gate. He could barely see it in the blackness of the moonless night; it stood out as darker in the darkness around him. A delicate breeze sifted past him, just enough to make the leaves rustle on the trees. The sound should have been normal and reassuring but instead it was ominous. Everything seemed ominous right now, in the deep of the night.

Alex put his hand on the gate and pushed. It didn't move. It was too much to ask that the gate be unlocked and open. He clicked on the miniature flashlight his mother had put on the keyring with his house key. "So you won't have to fumble around in the dark," she had told him, "You'll be safer this way." Alex had rolled his eyes at the time, but now he was glad it was here.

Carefully, shielding the tiny light from the view of the huge old house at the end of the driveway, he played the beam over the iron curlicues on the gate, looking for the best foot and handholds before he climbed over it. He frowned. Up close, he could see tiny skulls and skeletons hidden in the fancy rusted iron flourishes. There were faces, too - and not of anyone he'd ever care to meet, especially on a darker-than-dark night like this one.

He turned off the light and stood there for a minute. If he turned back now, he knew the guys would never let him forget it. He really didn't want to put up with the razzing...and he needed to be part of their group.

Jeremy's voice came back to him. "All you have to do, man, is go in and get the scarf I'm gonna tie to one of the tree limbs on that big old oak by the house. Then come back out and show me that you got it. Then you're in!" Jeremy had smiled then, his brilliant white teeth shining.

Oscar and Joe had nudged each other with their elbows and grinned, too. "Unless you don't think you can do that. And if you're scared, I understand, man. There's only been a few of us that did it, right, guys?" Oscar and Joe had nodded, looking important.

"And hey, remember, I have to go in and hang up that scarf every single time! So, you know, you're not the only one. I've done it again and again! But, you know, we're the best. Everybody knows we're not afraid of anything, and nobody - nobody - messes with us!" He had nodded emphatically at that, and Alex had nodded too.

He had liked the idea that no one would mess with him. He was the new guy, and sometimes that wasn't easy. He was always the new guy and he knew how it went. This looked like an easy in with a crowd that would keep him safe. And when school started again, that would be important.

He had questioned Jeremy, though. "What if the dude who owns the place has a gun? Some people shoot trespassers, don't they? And dogs? Are there any dogs?"

"The old guy who lives there is a distant relative of my dad's. He's grumpy, and he likes to be alone, but he won't do anything. Just don't go and mess around by the house, and you'll be fine. I mean, it's not like you're stealing or anything. You're just going to get a scarf that belongs to me. And he doesn't have dogs. Doesn't like animals." He had smiled sort of strangely at that. Then he said, "So what is it? Are you in?"

And Alex had said yes. And now he was skulking around this creepy gate, looking for a way over it and onto the property to retrieve the scarf that Jeremy had tied there earlier in the day. He knew where it was - they had all come by in the afternoon and Jeremy had pointed it out - a faint smudge of red dangling from the oak tree nearest the house. "Just jump up and yank it down, and come back out! And poof! You're in!"

It had seemed so much easier then. Even though the grounds were overgrown and looked like a snake factory and the very old house looked haunted and ready to tumble down, the light of day had made the idea of sneaking in and getting the scarf seem do-able. Even when Alex was sneaking out of the house after everyone else had gone to bed, it didn't seem so bad. But now, in the dark, dark night, Alex was ready to forget it and go back home to his warm soft bed and plug in the night light he had told his mother he didn't need anymore and listen to the radio until he fell asleep.

He slumped against the gate, smearing rust on the back of his shirt. He stood there for a few minutes and then, before he could think about it anymore, he grabbed the bars of the gate and swung himself up on them. Avoiding the spikes on the top, Alex clambered over and then he was panting, standing on the other side on the overgrown gravel drive.

Alex looked around. He was almost half-way done, he told himself. He just needed to run down the drive, grab the scarf, run back and get out. Then he could go home. And tomorrow, he could give the guys the scarf, his golden ticket to acceptance when the new school year started.

Except that he didn't run. He was too frightened. There was something about this place...there were no animal noises here and it just seemed spooky somehow. He crept down the drive, staying to the sides near the cover of the bushes, placing his feet carefully and trying not to make any noise at all. He slowed his breathing to quiet that down too, but he couldn't stop his heart from pounding so hard that he was sure someone could hear it three feet away. The hairs on the back of his neck were standing up, and every primeval instinct in his body was telling him to get out of here NOW!

The walk down the drive seemed to take forever. Alex startled and froze at each little sound he heard - the wind in the trees, a car out on the main road, something in the bushes nearby. When he finally reached the end of the drive and stood near the oak tree with the scarf, he was drenched in sweat and shaking with fear and he really couldn't say why. He stared at the house looming in front of him. Was that a flash of light he saw in the windows? No, but now he noticed that the breeze had stiffened and had blown up clouds. He could hear thunder booming in the distance. He needed to finish this; get the scarf and get away.

He could see the scarf dangling a few feet away and just out of arm's reach. One good jump and it would be his.

Alex gathered himself and leaped. As his hand wrapped around the fabric of the scarf and he pulled, something else wrapped around his legs, catching him and freezing him in mid-air.

Alex let out a screech that hurt even his own ears, feeling foolish even as he did it. It must be the guys, waiting here to scare him when he came in to get the scarf. He looked down, expecting to see Jeremy or Oscar or Joe with their arms around his legs, grinning up at him, laughing at him for screaming.

But it wasn't. What he saw made him scream again, this time until the breath ran all the way out of his body...

Dirty fangs in a hairy, filthy face. Arms the size of small trees. Eyes that glowed red in the night. And then the smell hit him, too. How he could have missed something that rank he didn't know. He gagged, and the thing holding him chuckled in a raspy bass voice.

"Well, what have we here? An interesting little morsel?! Come with me, morsel, and let's get acquainted!" The thing was carrying him towards the house as it spoke. Alex started wiggling and flailing his arms and trying to kick at the thing, screaming all the while.

Inside, the thing dumped him on the floor in a room with a single oil lamp and piles of rubbish everywhere. Alex instantly scuttled backwards until he hit a wall and huddled there, shaking, his eyes never leaving the thing that had grabbed him. He whimpered with every breath and could feel a growing dampness in his jeans pooling underneath him.

The thing watched him, an evil smile on its face. "So, little morsel, what do you think? What are you imagining right now? Because whatever you are imagining, I can make it come true. Your dreams, mind you, not your wishes. And only certain kinds of dreams at that. I believe your kind calls them nightmares?" He laughed again. "But first things first. I am forgetting my manners in my eagerness to get to know you better. I am Corrock. And you are...?"

Alex just stared at the thing. He pushed himself against the wall as if he were trying to push through it.

"Manners, morsel, manners! What is the matter with you? You'd think you never saw an ogre before! But then perhaps you haven't. I forget how uneducated and ignorant you modern youth are. The old ways, the old beings, have been forgotten." It shook its head and stared Alex right in the eyes. "I am an ogre. One of the last of my kind. I am bound to this estate and may not leave it. So my prey must come to me." He looked around the room and licked his lips. "I must say, I am ready for a change of diet. The local animals bore me." He looked around the room and Alex, following his gaze, could see piles of bones. There were squirrel skulls and deer skulls piled in a little heap nearby. He noticed the smell in the room for the first time and gagged again. Bile rose in the back of his throat.

Corrock laughed. "Good. The more scared they are, the juicier the flesh is when I finally get around to tasting it. I like it well seasoned with fear!"

Alex gasped and managed to croak, "M...my...my parents. They'll know I'm gone. They'll come and find me!" he finished in a rush.

"By now there should be a note in your room, in your handwriting, about how you didn't like it here and have run away. So sad, another runaway teenager who disappears. Oh my. He must have fallen in with the wrong crowd. Too bad, but it does happen," said the ogre in a grieving tone.

"A…a…a note?" His voice was hoarse from screaming.

"Didn't you wonder how the scarf could get here, without Jeremy, as he is calling himself these days, being caught by me? Jeremy and Oscar and Joe are mine. Think, morsel, did you ever go to their homes? Meet their families? No, you only saw them in public places. And had school begun, you'd never have seen them in school." It laughed, moving closer to Alex. "They bring me the young and the foolish, the lost and the desperate - anyone they can fool, in short - to stave off the pangs of my hunger."

"Many, many years ago, when I was first imprisoned here, these cocky young toughs decided to rob the place. I caught them, of course, and since I wasn't very hungry at the time, I made a bargain with them. They would bring me prey - tender, juicy young prey by preference, although I am not really picky - and I would let them live. It has worked well. They supply me with treats that I would not get otherwise and they are allowed to live - and live many more years than they should live by nature. In fact, they not only live, but have a glamour that allows them to seem any age they choose. I have been repaid many times over, and they get to live the lives they choose for the most part. It was a bargain well made." He smacked his lips in satisfaction and anticipation. The saliva dripping from his fangs glistened in the lamplight.

It was reaching for Alex who was cowering away when the sound of a door opening and closing stopped it. Footsteps echoed through the house and then Jeremy, Oscar and Joe entered the room. "Oh, you aren't done yet!" said Jeremy. "I thought you'd be finished by now. We'll wait outside. It gets a bit messy, you know." He winked and smirked at Alex. The trio suddenly seemed much older than they had. As the glamour that surrounded them faded away, they began to age before his eyes and now appeared ancient and evil. They all grinned wickedly at him with dirty, broken teeth in straggling and stained grey beards and Alex wondered why he hadn't seen how evil they were from the beginning.

The ogre said, "No, no - I think you should stay. You never stay for dinner. It's not very polite you know. You really should stay while I dine."

The three moved uneasily and their smiles died. "I insist," hissed the ogre.

"Right, sir. Whatever you say," they mumbled, trying to move to the door without seeming to.

The ogre turned back to Alex. While it had been talking to its three henchmen, Alex had been feeling around on the floor nearby. Now he had a squirrel skull in his hand and, before the ogre could reach for it again, Alex hurled the skull at the oil lamp.

The skull hit it with a smash and the oil from the lamp flew everywhere, bursting into flames as it did. Some of it splashed on the ogre, who roared in pain and rage. He whirled around, trying to reach the fire and put it out. Alex scrambled to his feet and ran toward the window, grabbing another bone as he went and throwing it against the glass.

The three in the doorway had rushed over to help their master, but when the glass in the window shattered they shouted and ran to stop Alex from escaping. In the confusion in the room, Jeremy got tangled up in a bone pile and fell to the floor, while Oscar got too close to the flames from the lamp and caught his clothing on fire. Joe was the only one left to pursue Alex and he was the farthest away, on the far side of the littered room.

The bone had broken the window, but the hole wasn't big enough for Alex to get through without slicing himself so badly that the ogre's work would be done for him. He swerved at the last minute and then ran through the door where the ogre's three cohorts had been standing a few minutes before. He could hear Joe shouting and then a crash that suggested that Joe had fallen into the remains of the window. He pelted down a dark and dirty hall - there was a door at the far end. He could see the window in it lighting up with the lightning from the storm that was almost upon them.

Alex raced to the door and yanked on the knob. It opened, and he nearly sobbed with relief. He was out onto the porch, dodging holes in the rotten boards, and then leaping down the steps in one leap. He was running for his life and he knew it. He listened for the sounds of pursuit behind him, but the shouts were still coming from inside the house. On an impulse, Alex swerved off the drive and into the bushes. He would find a tree and use it to get over the wall instead of going directly to the gate like they would expect.

The storm broke overhead. Rain poured down, drenching Alex in moments, and lightning flashed with thunder right on its heels. In the flashes, Alex navigated through the heavy growth. The rain masked the sound of his escape, but he knew it would also hide the sounds of anyone chasing him. He opted for speed instead of stealth and made for the wall as quickly as he could. There was a tree just the right size right by the wall and Alex swarmed up it as quickly as he could, expecting to feel arms pulling him back down at any moment.

He leapt from a tree branch to the top of the wall which he straddled, getting his balance. He looked back at the mansion. As he did, a slash of lightning came down from the clouds above and struck the oak tree that loomed beside the house. In the light from the lightning bolt, Alex could see one large and three small figures illuminated on the porch. And then the blazing branch from the tree came crashing down through the rotten porch roof onto the figures and setting the whole building ablaze. Alex could hear screams and roars echoing as he slipped from the wall, landing in the overflowing ditch beside it. Staggering to his feet, he ran all of the way home as if he could still feel the hot breath of the ogre behind him.

An article about the fire appeared in the local paper a few days later. There were some inquiries being made, it said, about all of the charred bones found in the ashes of the fire. Some in particular had been disturbingly strange. Alex could have told them why, but he wasn't sure they'd ever believe him...

Jane W. Wolfinbarger

THE LAUNDRY MONSTER

Anna couldn't pinpoint when things got quite so out of hand. One day, she was a load or two behind on the laundry, and the next there was a veritable Mt. Everest of laundry growing in the laundry room which quickly spread to the children's bedrooms.

"What is happening?" she moaned to her husband, as she brought yet another basket into the family room to fold.

He looked up from the television, confused. "What do you mean? People wear clothes, clothes get dirty, clothes need washing."

"Very funny. I mean, why is there so much, all of a sudden. Two weeks ago, I was caught up. Last week, there was some extra, but it didn't seem unreasonable. This week, it's all over the place. It's not like I've been skipping doing loads."

"You must've, or it wouldn't be out of hand. "

"Thank you, Mr. Logical."

"And all you have to do is an extra load or two a day until you catch up." His reasonable tone of voice was infuriating.

Anna dropped the basket of clean clothes in front of him. "Great. Then you must be volunteering to help fold some extra clothes. Have at it." She spun on her heel and stomped off to the laundry room to start another load.

Her husband, knowing when he was beat, quietly folded the basket of clothes.

Anna tried to catch up over the next few weeks, she really did, but nothing seemed to work. She taught the older children (who were certainly old enough to be useful) to do their own laundry, and gave everyone a laundry day. She herself did load after load, but the mountain of laundry didn't seem to get any smaller. If anything, it seemed to be growing. She sorted through and gave away all the outgrown clothes and the things no one would wear because they didn't like them, and she threw away all the clothes and linens with holes and stains. She pared everyone's wardrobe down to the point that closets and drawers began to look naked. Yet the pile still grew.

Her neighbor, Edna Reynolds, whose house always looked like a magazine photo shoot was going to show up at any minute, dropped by one morning, recruiting for the PTA fair. Anna was in the middle of folding yet another load of laundry. Anna had forgotten to close the laundry room door when she ran to answer the doorbell, and Edna, of course, had radar for messes. "You know, I was reading just yesterday about some internet programs designed to help people get organized," Edna said very sweetly with a barely concealed smirk on her face. "Not that I need them of course, but I understand they can be very helpful."

"Thanks," Anna grated. She bared her teeth in what she hoped would be taken as a smile.

Snatching the sign-up sheet, she put her name under a random booth that she would no doubt regret later, and all but shoved Edna out the door, locking it behind her. She put her head in her hands and moaned. Edna was the sort of person who came over, made remarks that weren't nearly as nice as they sounded, and then went and told the whole neighborhood bad things about your housekeeping. Muttering things under her breath that, if anyone had heard her, would have greatly enriched the household cussing jar, Anna slammed the door to the laundry room, and locked it, too. Anna took refuge in the knowledge that Edna's children were horrible little brats and decided that the best idea for now was denial. She spent the rest of the morning out running errands.

However, the laundry problem had to be solved, and now the business with Edna had brought it to a head. The technique of grabbing a load off the top of the pile and washing it, then repeating with the next load, clearly wasn't working with this monstrous pile of washing.

Anna broke down, withdrew a considerable chunk of cash from the ATM and had her husband take the whole lot to the laundromat one Saturday. (He got black looks from the students who were regulars when he monopolized most of the machines.) He and the children sorted them, folded them, dropped a load of give-aways by the second-hand charity on the way home, and put away all of the clothing in the baskets. They all smiled victoriously and went out for ice cream to celebrate.

On Monday, Anna went into the laundry room to gloat, humming happily. The only laundry she had was the small basket with clothing from the bathroom hamper that she was taking into the laundry room with her. She stopped short on the threshold and gasped. The pile was back, as if it had never left, where there had been emptiness the day before.

Horrified, she ran to check the children's closets and drawers to see if they had emptied them into her clean laundry room as some sort of practical joke. The drawers and closets were still full though, and she saw some cloth arms and legs sneaking out from under the children's beds where there had been none the day before.

Now, Anna was a practical and down to earth sort of woman. She believed in what she could see and touch, and didn't indulge herself in fantasy. But even she could see that something strange was going on here. There was no way that pile could be back without some kind of uncanny help.

Anna went out into the laundry room and, steeling herself against the squishy sorts of things that she sometimes encountered in the children's laundry, plunged her arm into the middle of the pile, pulling out an item at random. It appeared to be a stained, outgrown shirt that had belonged to the oldest child when he was a toddler. She grabbed at another. It was a skirt that she knew she had put in the Salvation Army box because her daughter refused to wear it.

She grabbed a basket and put these things in it and grabbed a few more. Everything was old, outgrown, or – she could swear - given away. There were even a few things she didn't recognize at all, including some single socks that were unlike anything she had ever purchased. (She would never buy chartreuse socks with little pink bunnies on them - not in this life time, anyway.) Anna piled all of her evidence in the laundry basket behind her.

When she thought she had a basket full, she turned around to grab it and take it - somewhere, maybe to the garbage - and the basket was empty. There was nothing in it, not even the pair of pale pink size 44 boxer shorts she had just put in it. Anna looked slowly back to the pile, which was the same size as ever (or was it bigger?) and then back at the now empty basket again. She slowly backed out of the room, shut the door tight and then ran to her bedroom. She spent the rest of the day in bed, with the pillows over her head.

When the children came home from school, they tried to get her to tell them what was wrong, but all she did was moan quietly. The children tiptoed around for the rest of the afternoon and made peanut butter and jelly sandwiches for supper. When their dad came home, they made him one, too.

The next day, Anna had recovered. She decided that the day before had been a figment of her imagination. She marched back out to the laundry room with not one, but three baskets in her hands - one for darks, one for lights, and one for bleach whites. She had an uneasy moment when she first saw the pile - was it really bigger?- but she sternly told herself not to be a ninny and started grabbing clothing off the top of the pile and sorting it into baskets.

"Lights, lights, darks, bleach, darks…." She muttered the litany of laundry to herself to keep herself from thinking. She didn't even examine the things she found - they were probably just hand me downs from friends anyway - she just put them into baskets to wash. When she turned back around, the baskets were all full. She smiled contentedly and put the first load in the washer. "There, now, that was easy, wasn't it," she told herself reassuringly.

That load went into the dryer and the next went into the washer and all was still going properly. She folded up the first load, reloaded both washer and dryer and things were still going along swimmingly.

Anna was humming to herself when she put the clean clothes away and added items to the give-away box. These were all things she recognized, mostly clothes the children had worn over the last week. All was well.

All was well, that is, until she went to start the fourth load. That was when the trouble started.

Anna had just started to fill another set of three baskets. Again, she wasn't watching what went into them too carefully, but some of it seemed pretty strange, even if the items were hand-me-downs from the neighbors. She filled the baskets and turned around to grab the first one for the washer. The one with lights in it was empty. The one with darks in it was half empty. Only the one with bleach whites had the proper amount of laundry in it. And as she watched, the level of laundry in the basket of darks slowly dropped, like water in a tub when someone has pulled the plug.

With Anna standing there staring at it, the basket emptied, and the basket of bleach whites began to do the same thing. Anna's eyes were like saucers. She gulped, and finally realized she could move. She took a deep breath and screamed. Loudly. Then she ran from the laundry room, slammed the door, locked it and ran to the garage for some two-by-fours. Five minutes later, the door to the laundry room was nailed shut.

She called her husband at work. As soon as he picked up the phone, she said, without preamble, "The laundry room is haunted."

Her husband replied, "What?"

"It's haunted. The laundry room is haunted. That's why we can't seem to make headway against the laundry. It's haunted and whatever is in there is sucking in the laundry and keeping it there. Some of it isn't even ours. I mean, you don't wear size 44 pink boxers. And certainly the boys don't. They're way too little."

"Uh-huh. What was that you said? Sorry, I was in the middle of something. Now tell me again. I could have sworn you said the laundry room was haunted."

Anna snarled incoherently, slammed the phone down and stormed off to the bedroom, where she spent the rest of the day watching old movies on TV and mumbling to herself. When the children came home from school, she took them straight back out again, first to the park and then to their favorite fast food burger place.

When they came home several hours later, they found her husband in front of the laundry room door. The boards that Anna had put up were pried off, but a new set had been nailed up, and a cross was hung on the door, too.

"I came home early," he explained. "You sounded so upset on the phone, I thought I'd better see what was going on. I took down the boards you had up, and went out there myself. I tried to start a load of laundry, but the basket was empty before I could put it into the washer. Then I watched the pile - grow." He turned pale and gulped. "It grew, right in front of my eyes." He turned to his wife with an earnest look. "I am so sorry. I thought, well, I thought that you were imagining things. But you weren't. There's something out there." He looked at the door and shuddered.

Anna shook her head and said, "No, I don't blame you. I thought it was my imagination, too. But what are we going to do!?"

The children had been watching the exchange with interest. The oldest one said, "A haunted room! COOL! But does it have to be the laundry room? That's kind of lame. It would be better if it was the attic or something!"

The next one down wasn't so sure. "I don't like ghosts," he said.

The littlest one said, "It's probably the monster under my bed. He hasn't been there lately. He must have moved to the laundry room."

Anna started to say something and stopped. Her husband started to say something and stopped. The older children looked thoughtful. Finally Anna said, "If we accept the idea that there's something - strange - in the laundry room, then maybe a monster under the bed isn't such a far-fetched idea after all."

She handed her husband the bag containing the burger and fries they had brought home for him (they were cold now) and looked thoughtfully at the door. Then she turned to the littlest one and said, "Honey, you need to tell us everything you know about the monster under your bed."

For the rest of the evening, they picked the brains of the littlest one about the monster under her bed. When the older ones admitted that the monster had plagued them when they were smaller (actually they pointed out that their parents had dismissed their complaints as products of over-active imaginations), they were included in the inquisition.

By bedtime, at least none of them were panicking any more. They took down the boards (but left the cross) to take one more look and found a few new clothes on the top of the heap. Then they shut the door tight again.

That night, the littlest one came out of her bedroom complaining that the monster under her bed was back. "Well, I guess it wasn't the monster from under her bed," Anna said to her husband.

For the rest of the week, Anna simply shuttled the dirty clothes to the laundromat. She found that if she grabbed them quickly enough, the clothes did not migrate out to the laundry room. She was making daily laundry runs.

On Tuesday, she grabbed a drill and made a peephole in the laundry room door so she could keep track of what was happening in there. She really wished she hadn't, because the pile was larger than ever.

On Wednesday, Edna from across the street came over again, this time with the instructions for the booth Anna had signed up for. It was, just as Anna had predicted, the worst one there was. "I've noticed you've been going to the laundromat an awful lot lately, my dear. Still having trouble with your laundry? Is your machine out? Can I help in any way?"

Anna smiled quietly, took the instructions, and just said, "We're waiting on parts."

On her way out, Edna managed to walk by the laundry room. A sleeve was crawling out from under the door, clearly trying to escape the horror within. Edna reached over and open the door to push the shirt back in. Anna cringed, but it was too late. The huge pile, towering over the washer and dryer was displayed in all its glory. Edna simply raised her eyebrows, smiled slightly, and said, "As I said, dear, if you need help, just let me know. I can give you the name of a personal organizer." and walked away with a triumphant swish in her step.

At dinner that night, Anna told her family about Edna. The littlest one was sympathetic - the Reynolds children had been picking on her on the playground again. The older children looked at each other when they heard that and the oldest one simply said, "Don't worry, I think they'll stop soon," and then they all burst into giggles. Anna was suspicious, but couldn't get anything else out of them. She and her husband spent the rest of the evening trying to figure out what to do about the laundry.

By Friday, she had had enough of everything. At dinner that night, she told her family, "Enough is enough. Tomorrow we are taking back our laundry room."

At eight o'clock on Saturday morning, the entire family gathered by the laundry room door. They had basket upon basket, and the oldest child had a big butterfly net. They marched into the laundry room and everyone began filling baskets as quickly as they could. The baskets were once again mysteriously emptying as they were being filled, but with everyone working together to clear the pile, they were being filled faster than they emptied.

Gradually, the family neared the bottom. The oldest child, with the butterfly net at the ready, got on one side of the pile, and everyone else grabbed the last few pieces of laundry. At the bottom was a tiny animated figure, still covered by a sheet. They couldn't see much, but it clearly had very long arms and a tiny body. The oldest child quickly slammed the butterfly net down on top of the figure and scooped it up. The bundle in the net squirmed and wriggled, and several more pieces of laundry expanded the net, but the laundry monster did not escape.

Quickly, Anna's husband took the lid off a five gallon bucket he had ready for just this purpose and the oldest child dipped the net into the bucket. His father slammed the lid down as Anna clipped the net from the handle. The bucket bounced a little and then settled down. They all looked at the laundry pile expectantly, but nothing changed. They waited. It didn't grow any larger.

Anna hefted the bucket experimentally. It wiggled a little bit. Whatever had been in the laundry pile was definitely in the bucket now. Anna's husband grabbed some duct tape and taped the lid down securely - just in time, too, because several items of clothing vanished from the floor and the lid to the bucket began to bulge.

"Well, it looks like it can bring things to it, but not get itself out," said Anna. "Hopefully." She rapped on the wooden door frame for luck.

"What are you going to do with it?" asked the middle child.

"I don't know yet," answered his father. "Let's go get some breakfast and think about it."

Later that morning, Anna went out to the laundry room and the bucket was gone. She was moving things around, looking for it, when the oldest child came along and said, "Oh, don't worry. I took care of it. It won't bother you anymore!" and then ran away giggling. She couldn't get anything else out of him.

At lunch, Anna said to the youngest one, "I guess the monster under your bed is next."

The littlest one answered, "It's gone now. We got rid of it." Again the children looked at each other and laughed.

The next afternoon while they were getting in the car to go to the park, Anna and the children saw Edna Reynolds, looking very cross, coming out of her house with a full laundry basket on her hip and a crying child following her. Anna heard her saying, "I don't want to hear anything about monsters under your bed. I want to know where all this laundry came from! Have you been hiding it somewhere? I'm going to have to go to the laundromat to catch this stuff up!"

Anna looked in the back seat at her children, who sat there with their hands stuffed in their mouths trying not to laugh out loud. She started to say something, and then shook her head and stopped. Instead, she stuck her head out of the car window, smiled, and called sweetly, "Can I help with anything, Edna?"

DON'T FORGET YOUR CHANGE

"Creepy little guy," Marge said as she and I were sitting down with lattes at the coffee shop near my new house while I took a break from painting and scraping wallpaper. The man in question was staring at me and smiling slightly. "He looks like he escaped from someone's Halloween party - or maybe the set of a horror movie." She gave a delicate shudder.

"Yeah, I know. And weird as it seems, I keep seeing him everywhere. I would almost say he was following me, except that...well, I did just move into this neighborhood, and I don't know everyone's movement patterns. He could have legitimate business being the same places I am." I paused for a mouthful of caramel latte and shrugged. "I mean, it's not like he's been hanging around my house or anything. I've just seen him in lots of public places. He is sort of hard to miss. Still, I'm glad you saw him too. I've tried to point him out to Hank, but he claims he hasn't spotted him."

"Hard to miss? I guess! I mean, four foot six, hair like a huge bunch of grey spider webs standing on end, and a nose you could almost go fishing with? And that complexion – I don't think I've ever seen that shade of grey outside of a black and white movie! Not to mention the funky suit. He looks like he just stepped out of some movie set in Victorian times, or maybe Victorian times themselves because both he and the suit look that old! And it's nowhere near Halloween!" Marge never was one to avoid speaking her mind.

"It is an older neighborhood and a lot of the houses are Victorians. Maybe he just likes to dress to match the architecture," I joked.

Marge glared at me. "I don't buy that for a minute, and neither do you. If I thought that guy was following me, I'd be filing a complaint with the cops yesterday!" She shook her head.

"I'll see about it if I keep seeing him, or if he starts coming closer." Then I changed the subject, asking about people in the neighborhood where I used to live, and where Marge still did. That kept her occupied the rest of the morning.

I did notice the little man around a lot in the next few days, but then I started noticing other people more too, and decided his daily routine just happened to coincide with mine.

A few days later, my new next door neighbor, Susie, asked me over for a glass of iced tea after we were done with our yard work. "Come on over – you look wiped out. Not used to such big lots, are you?" Susie wiped her own perspiring face and took off her gloves.

"No, but I like your idea for a break!" I climbed over the low iron fence and joined her in her kitchen.

"So, how do you like the neighborhood?" Susie asked me over iced tea and cookies. Her kids kept buzzing through to tank up on cookies for a mid-morning snack.

"I love it! It's just beautiful and all the people seem so nice! And Hank and I are loving restoring our house!" I enthused. I wasn't just saying it, either; I really did like the neighborhood. It was an eclectic mix of people from all backgrounds and walks of life. The houses were a mix, too, with restored Victorians like Hank's and mine rubbing shoulders with little 1930's bungalows and the occasional 50's ranch. "I especially like the way the whole neighborhood is built around the park. It gives it a sort of old fashioned flair. I've been walking the dog in the park almost every evening, and I just love it!"

One of Susie's kids was raiding the cookie jar. He turned to me and said, "Are you throwing your penny in the pond when you walk over the bridge at night?" He looked straight at me and added, "Don't forget, 'cause it's big trouble if you do!"

Susie looked at me and shrugged. "The kids say that after dark, you have to throw a penny in the pond when you cross the bridge, otherwise the troll will get you. I don't know. I've never tossed in a penny, and the troll hasn't gotten me yet!" She smiled.

The boy didn't smile. He looked at her seriously and said, "That's 'cause one of us always goes the next day and throws in a dime. If you don't pay right away, it costs more. He'll give you 'til the next day, though, just in case you had to cross the bridge and were broke." He looked back at me. "Us kids always pay for our parents the next day." He shrugged.

"Well, it's your pocket money!" laughed Susie. "Besides, I don't think I've ever heard of the troll getting anyone and there are plenty of people who don't toss in pennies!"

The boy shook his head. "He'll let you by if you're just visiting. If you live in the neighborhood, he figures you ought to know better. And what about Old Man Summers?"

"Excuse me?" said his mother pointedly.

"Sorry. Mister Summers. He disappeared, and he wouldn't ever pay the troll. He was way too stingy!"

Susie opened her mouth to say something to her son, then stopped and sighed, rolling her eyes. She turned to me. "Joe Summers disappeared during that cold snap last winter.

He was getting a bit senile and we think he just wandered off. But the kids, you know, they have to embroider everything."

Her son just looked at her and shook his head. Then he turned to me again, "Well, anyway, if you haven't been paying, then you should start. And give him something extra, 'cause he doesn't like it if people owe him money!" He jammed a cookie in his mouth and bounced out the back door.

"Sorry about that!" Susie said. "Now you know some of our neighborhood folklore. The kids really seem to take it seriously, though!"

Talk drifted away to other topics and I sort of forgot about it. Over the next few weeks, though, I did notice, without really thinking about it, that a lot of people, adults and children alike, tended to toss pennies from the bridge into the pond.

I kept seeing the strange little man here and there, but it wasn't until the end of the month that he started to get closer. I noticed him one day when I was leaving the grocery store. I was juggling with several bags - I thought I wouldn't need the cart to take them to the car, and I was wrong - and he came up beside me.

"Here, let me take one of those for you," he said, in a low voice. Somehow, he managed to sound scary just offering to help. He took a bag just as I was about to drop it, and I noticed that his fingernails were yellowed and thick, almost like claws. When he handed the bag back to me at the car, he touched the receipt at the top of the bag and said, "All paid for, right and proper, eh?"

Before I could reply to this cryptic statement, he turned and left.

A few days later I was out weeding flower beds. I had my dog tied to a tree nearby to keep me company. A fence high enough to keep him in was on the list of things to do, but way down near the bottom under things like fixing the bathrooms. In the meantime, Jasper got tied up when he was outside.

Jasper woofed at something behind me. I stood up, turned around and saw that the man was on the sidewalk, looking at me. I stared back at him, and he tipped his hat and smiled at me, showing a lot of broken, brown teeth. "Walking your nice dog later, are you?" he asked. Then he quickly walked by while I was still thinking of an answer. I untied the dog and we spent the afternoon inside.

That night I gave Hank the rundown on what was going on. He shook his head and said, "I can see why you're creeped out, but I don't think there's anything we can do about it at this point. He's probably just the neighborhood eccentric."

"I would think Susie would have said something."

"Maybe they just take him for granted. You can ask her tomorrow."

"Next week. They took the kids to the mountains for a week."

"Lucky them!" said Hank, yawning, and he rolled over to go to sleep.

I stayed awake for a little while, thinking. It really was strange.

The next day, I was walking the dog on a little path on the edge of the park. Jasper saw a squirrel and lunged with all his Labrador might, yanking me off my feet and pulling me over onto my front. I skidded and rolled, ending up half under a park bench. As I cussed and tried to wiggle my way out again with the apologetic dog making a nuisance out of himself, I heard someone come up behind me.

"Here, let me give you a hand," said a familiar low voice. The dog was pulled off of me, and I rolled over onto my back. The little man reached down as if to take my hand to help me up, and then stopped and leaned in close to me. "Debts that are not paid promptly increase exponentially," he hissed at me sibilantly. "Interest, you know." He smiled, once again showing a mouthful of broken brown teeth. His breath wasn't quite fetid. Not quite. Then he took my hand and lifted me to my feet with a strength that was astonishing. The dog whined and stuck himself to my side like he was glued there. The man handed back the leash, tipped his hat and hurried off in the other direction, leaving me standing there with my mouth open once again. I went straight home and locked the doors.

I didn't see the man around for a while, and decided that he must have been committed somewhere or something. It might also have had something to do with the fact that I found plenty of work inside to occupy my time until I began to feel safe again, although I was still giving the park a wide berth. I kept forgetting to ask Susie about him, but it didn't seem to matter anymore.

One evening, Hank and I had Marge and a few other friends from the old neighborhood over for dinner and to show off our freshly-redone home. After dinner and lots of admiring of the house, everyone decided they would like to take a walk in the park. It was a beautiful autumn evening, perfect for a walk. As we were leaving, Marge asked about the creepy little man and I replied, "He's still around, and still really creepy. But he never seems to bother me when other people are around, so we should be okay."

We walked along the paths and chatted. The leaves lay all over the ground and a few last flowers grew in the beds. The air was clean and fresh with just a hint of wood smoke - the perfect evening for a walk. We made our way up to the pond, and started over the bridge. One of our guests stopped and reached into his pocket for a coin, and tossed it into the pond.

"Making a wish?" asked Marge.

"I guess. I just know that whenever I've been here, people are throwing coins in the pond." He laughed a little.

I said, "The neighborhood kids say they are paying the troll." Everyone laughed at that, and a few others tossed in some coins - just for luck, they said. We kept walking, but I thought I saw something moving near the edge of the pond as we left. When I turned around, there was nothing there.

A few days later, the dog got out of the front door and cleared the low fence with one bound. (We finally had a good fence in back, so he didn't try to get out that door.) With me hard on his furry heels, he made a beeline for the park and the squirrels he dreamed of catching.

I finally caught up with him over by the pond. As I slipped the leash on him, I heard someone come up behind me. It was Mr. Creepy again. He smiled that revolting smile and hissed, "I know you wouldn't want your debts to go into collections. Collections tend to be very unpleasant. And their fees are so high. You might just need to give up some of your most precious possessions to pay them off."

That did it. I screamed. I screamed loud and long, and ran home as fast as I could. I locked the door and then I called the police.

The policeman who came was very polite. He took my report and then said he'd be on the lookout for the man. He thought he might have seen him before but he really wasn't sure. He hadn't worked in this neighborhood for very long. That did not make me feel much better - this guy was hard to miss. After the policeman left, I huddled in the living room, thinking.

Later that evening I updated Hank on the day's events. He shook his head and said, "Yeah, I haven't heard anything about an eccentric old man, either. The only creepy thing I could find out was that every now and then someone drowns in that pond. Sad, but not really sinister, especially as old as that pond is. Something bad is bound to happen occasionally."

I wasn't so sure about that.

That night I started hearing...things... bumping around outside the house. Hank swore he didn't hear anything, but then he could sleep through a loggers' convention. I checked around outside the next day, but nothing was out of place. Finally, after thinking it over for a while, I took five silver dollars from the stash I kept for that trip to Las Vegas that Hank and I kept talking about taking. I put Jasper on his leash and walked over to the pond. Taking a deep breath, I walked carefully out on the bridge and closed my eyes and dropped the coins into the water. Nothing happened, and I walked home feeling foolish.

That night the bumping continued, and it sounded like someone was trying the knobs on the doors. Once again, Hank didn't wake up. I pulled the covers over my head and tried to sleep.

The next morning, when I let the dog back in the house after his morning outing in the back yard, I saw something tucked under his collar. I pulled out a small piece of paper with spidery old-fashioned script on it. I blanched when I read it. "Too little too late," it said.

That day I stayed inside all day, keeping the dog at my side.

I showed the note to Hank when he got home. "Probably just one of the neighborhood kids playing a joke on you."

"That writing doesn't look like any kid's writing," I said.

"Kids can take calligraphy classes, too," Hank said rationally. "Even kids that play jokes on people."

That night the bumping outside started early and was loud enough that even Hank noticed it. Jasper was barking and running from window to window.

Hank snarled and hauled up the bedroom window. He leaned out and shouted, "Cut it out! Or I'll tell your parents!" He turned to me. "Probably just those same kids playing pranks. It happens."

He yawned. "Ask around the neighborhood tomorrow, or file a report with the police."

Things quieted down and Hank went right back to sleep. Jasper and I stayed awake for quite a while, though, jumping at every sound.

I asked around the neighborhood the next day, but no one knew anything. Susie was a little upset. She hadn't heard the ruckus, but she figured that if someone was bothering us, she might be next. She offered to put out more feelers to see what she could find out.

The next night, the bumping started again. I called the cops, and while they drove by the house and promised to keep an eye on the house that night, they didn't see anything or anyone suspicious. The sounds settled down after that, and we fell asleep.

About midnight, things changed. A rock flew through the bedroom window, and laughter came from the yard below.

"That does it!" Hank hauled on his jeans, trying to avoid stepping on the broken glass, and stomped down the stairs. Jasper ran in circles around him, barking.

I followed, saying, "Just call the police and let it go, Hank. I don't think this is safe."

"I'm just going to go out on the porch and see if I can see any of the little monsters," he said. "I won't do anything stupid. Maybe I can scare them off."

Jasper stood in front of the door, barking. But he wasn't barking at the door. He was barking at Hank, trying to keep him from opening the door. Hank pushed past him and went out on the porch. I hung back, my hand through Jasper's collar, afraid of what I might see.

I heard Hank say something, and then I heard a loud thump followed by silence. I peered out the window and didn't see Hank on the porch.

"Hank?" There was silence. I leaned out the door to look. Jasper whined.

I didn't see Hank anywhere.

Then, in the distance, I heard a yell. It sounded like Hank, and it sounded like it was coming from near the park.

A thousand scenarios of what might have happened ran through my mind at once. "You might just need to give up some of your most precious possessions," hissed the voice in my memory. And, "What about Old Man Summers?" and "every now and then someone drowns in that pond."

"NO!" I screamed in horror. "NO! YOU CAN'T HAVE HIM!"

I tore up the stairs and dumped the contents of my jewelry box on the bed. I pawed through the pile and grabbed the one good piece of jewelry I had, a diamond and ruby broach that had been my grandmother's. With Jasper in the lead, I almost tumbled down the stairs in my haste and then bolted over to the park as fast as I could. I could hear my blood pounding in my ears as I raced through the darkness.

Through the still night, I could hear a few more shouts that sounded like Hank, and then, as I approached the middle of the park, nothing.

"HANK! HANK!" I screamed so loudly my voice was raw. There was no answer, but I knew where I needed to go. I raced for the pond and the bridge.

When I got there, the normally still water was all churned up, like something had just been thrown into it. Jasper ran over to something on the bank and nosed it. It was a slipper that looked like one of the pair I had given Hank for Christmas last year and it was soaking wet.

I pounded up onto the bridge, my feet thumping hollowly on the boards, and flung the broach down into the water screaming, "GIVE HIM BACK!"

There was silence. Complete silence. No crickets, no sleepy chirps from birds, no wind in the bare branches overhead. Jasper was sitting silently on the bank, staring at the water. Even the waves on the pond went still. It went on so long that I thought I had been a complete fool and Hank would be at home wondering where I was and why my jewelry was everywhere.

Then a whisper came out of nowhere, "Paid in full."

There was a loud splashing and suddenly Hank was staggering out of the pond beside Jasper, coughing and gasping for breath. I ran to him and threw my arms around him, crying. We clung together there for a few minutes with Jasper whining and licking at both of us, and then the three of us staggered home.

We talked about what had happened for the rest of the night. The one thing that came out of the conversation was that we were moving - to another town - as soon as possible.

The next day I simply told Susie that the kids were right and to toss money in the pond when she used the bridge. She looked at me like I was crazy, and kept her distance after that. I couldn't imagine what she would have said if I had told her the whole story.

I gave her kids the rest of my silver dollar stash and told them to use it to pay for their mom and anyone else who needed it. They thanked me very seriously, and I saw them putting the money in a can under the porch to hide it from Susie. At least they believed me.

We sold our beloved dream Victorian at a loss. When we moved out, I left a note for the people who bought our lovely home that said to make sure to make a wish and toss a penny in the pond every time they used the bridge after dark. I also left a coffee can full of pennies for them for just that purpose.

The day we left, I noticed Jasper growling and staring at the front door. Looking out on the porch, I found a small package. It contained a single ruby and a note in a familiar spidery handwriting.

The note read, "Don't forget your change."

A few years later we read an article in the paper that said someone else had drowned in the pond and the city had decided to drain it and fill it in because it was just too dangerous. They found it odd, the article said, that they found hardly any coins in the bottom of the pool; people had been throwing them in for so long, there should have been a small fortune there. Hank and I weren't surprised. And we still toss coins from bridges into ponds and streams when we cross over them, especially at night - just in case.

Jane W. Wolfinbarger

DRAGON, PARTY OF TWO

"Dragon, Party of Two…"

The hostess' voice was hard to distinguish over the noise in the bar. However, Yuri Farmer tilted his head and lifted his glass of 30-year-old Scotch. He took the arm of his date, who picked up her martini, and caught the eye of the hostess searching the crowded room.

"I believe that's us," he said to his date, who was wearing a sheath dress clinging to her every curve in her signature color white. Yuri held her close to him as he navigated the room to follow the hostess.

"Dragon? Now why would you use that name?" his date purred, raising her eyebrows and smiling suggestively.

"Why not?" Yuri replied with a slight smile, his eyes cool and his feet sure in the crowd.

His date allowed herself a small smirk and followed him. Yuri was considered quite a catch in certain circles – handsome, intelligent, and, above all, rich. This was supposed to be a business meeting, but she intended to turn it into something else. And what Janine Delarosa wanted, she usually got.

With dinner ordered and an appropriate wine chosen, they settled down to enjoy appetizers (caviar was her choice) and conversation.

"So, Miss Delarosa," he began, but she interrupted.

"Janine, please," she smiled invitingly. "And may I call you Yuri?"

"Of course," Yuri replied and continued, "I understand that you have held the position of vice president for five years now? You are in charge of acquiring new accounts, are you not?"

"What is this, an inquisition?" But her tone and the smile playing across her lips took the edge off the question.

"Not at all. But if I am going to do business with your company, I want to make sure I have all of the details correct. This is a business meeting, so if I intend to write it off on taxes, I need to do at least a little business." He met her eyes, smiling. "So why don't you tell me a bit about yourself?"

Janine's smile grew larger, and if possible, a bit predatory, and she obliged. "I've held the position of VP for five years, yes, and yes, I am in charge of the acquisition of new accounts. I worked my way up through the ranks of the company in what they say is record time – I seem to have a talent for acquisitions." She paused to take a small bite of the caviar. "But then, I do enjoy the work, and I enjoy the finer things in life that go along with success."

"I understand," Yuri replied. "To the finer things in life," and he raised his wine glass for a toast.

Glasses clinked and the conversation continued – witty repartee, compliments, partial truths, detail carefully avoided – the evening was a tribute to attempted seduction and the finer things in life.

Janine managed to avoid mentioning the three husbands, each richer than the last, that she had left in her wake in the last ten years, and the people whom she had stepped on in her precipitous climb to VP. She did not mention that she had the CEO position in her sights, but it was understood by anyone who knew her.

For Yuri's part, there was a lot left out, and most of what was said was fabrication, either partial or of the whole cloth.

After the last bit of dessert was scraped from the plate and the last of the after-dinner coffee was sipped, the valet retrieved Yuri's Lexus from the parking lot and Janine was securely tucked into the passenger seat.

"Your place or mine?" Yuri asked, locking his eyes with hers.

"Oh, mine," she purred. "I think you'll like it. And we can go for a lovely walk by the lake – in the moonlight." Her smile promised more than a walk.

Yuri smiled back and aimed the car towards the lake.

They did walk along the shore, while wavelets washed against the sand with quiet swishes and crickets chirped a few steps away in the trees. It was lonely and quiet, and they talked about art and music and things that they enjoyed. Yuri, against his wishes, found himself being charmed by Janine in a way that no woman had charmed him in years. She let it slip that she contributed to a charity of which Yuri was a board member. He was surprised to hear this.

"My dear, I am pleased that you find it such a good charity," he told her.

"Yuri, I haven't always been this wealthy. My father left us when I was small, and my mother and I had to make do. I remember going to bed hungry," she said. "I don't like to remember it, but I can't seem to forget," she said with a small grimace. "And don't you dare tell anyone about it. It will ruin my image of a hard-hearted bitch."

Yuri laughed and made a mental note to check and see if she truly did support the charity.

Philanthropy did not fit with the woman he suspected her to be.

Shortly after that, Yuri excused himself. "My dear, this has been wonderful, but I have an early flight to catch tomorrow. I'll be out of town for a week, but when I come back, I'd love to take up where we left off." He embraced her and kissed her gently on the forehead in promise.

Janine smiled seductively. "I'll bet you would. Well, so would I. And you never did tell me why you used the name Dragon," she added.

"When I get back." He walked her to her door. She stood outside watching him as he left.

Yuri was confused. It never went like this – never. He never had feelings for women like Janine. He never had feelings for women anymore, anyway; at least not since his wife had died. No woman could ever take her place, and he had made sure not to let any woman since slip into his heart, especially one like Janine. She was business and needed to remain business.

He shook his head angrily. He needed to get his head back in the game, or bad things could happen. He tore his mind from Janine's smile and her warm curves, reminded himself of the people she had stepped on to get to the top, and then turned his thoughts to the next day. St. Louis. Yuri needed to think about how he was going to handle things in St. Louis.

St. Louis was hot and steamy, but his business contact there lived to play golf when he wasn't in the boardroom making a killing. Golf suited Yuri's purposes perfectly, and he agreed to an afternoon round.

The man was abominable. Greedy didn't even begin to describe him. He made his fortune on the backs of the desperate, stopping at no one or nothing to get what he wanted. Yuri knew for certain that he brought in women from other places – impoverished places – telling them that they would be mail-order brides, and then using them as prostitutes. He bought and sold people as if they were livestock, and when he used up one, he disposed of them and got two more in their place. He wore a mask of respectability, but Yuri knew what he really was.

As they played and Yuri forced himself to make small talk with this prince of industry and king of deception, the clouds gathered overhead. Yuri had made sure to keep the game close. He knew that the man could not stand to lose, and would want to finish the game no matter what.

When they reached the middle of the back nine, the rain started and thunder growled. And as Yuri had predicted, his partner did not want to stop playing. He was just a few strokes ahead of Yuri, and was compelled to win above all else. The rest of the course was empty when Yuri made his move.

He slipped an object out of his golf bag. It was about the size of a skein dhu, a small knife traditionally worn by a Scotsman in his sock, but where the blade should be there was an ancient curve of pointed ivory. As the other man stood after his swing, tracking the ball, Yuri slipped up behind him and pricked the tip of the thing into the back of the man's arm.

"Hey, what the hell?!" the man swung around angrily, golf club raised to strike. Yuri was out of range, though, having danced back immediately after the jab. "You son of a bitch, what did you just do?!"

A trickle of blood ran down to the man's elbow and dripped off. "You'll see in just a moment," Yuri replied calmly. And something was certainly happening. The blood dripping was changing color, darkening and becoming more viscous. The man himself seemed to be enlarging and changing shape.

Yuri watched impassively as the man screamed. It was just as he had predicted. He had been wrong once or twice over the years, but certainly not recently. The man's shape wavered, grew, and wavered again. Yuri glanced overhead at the clouds. They were just about perfect. Just a few more minutes….

Finally the change was complete, and on the golf course of the exclusive club in the middle of America, just where the industrial tycoon had been, stood a very large black dragon.

The dragon roared, the sound blending with the thunder overhead. It looked down at its new form and raised its wings experimentally. "This is wonderful!" Its voice threatened to break Yuri's eardrums. "I should thank you for reminding me of who I was. All those years in that weak human form, and I had forgotten myself." The wedge-shaped head snaked down to Yuri's level.

"Who are you, and why did you return me to my native form?" it asked. "What was that thing you stuck me with, puny human?"

Yuri, with an eye to the clouds, stalled for time. "A dragon's tooth," he said, "enchanted to bring out a dragon's true form. I pried it from the jaw of the dragon who murdered my wife, after I killed him." He raised his arms. "As for who I am, I am Yuri Farmer." He laughed. "I have had other names throughout the ages: Jason, Sigurd, Gilgamesh and St. George. And as for what I do - I rid the world of the greed of dragons."

With this he said something in a tongue long dead, and light poured down from the clouds, a lightning bolt shaped like a sword blade that sped straight into the heart of the dragon. A huge snap and then a boom laid Yuri out flat on his back. When he looked up, the dragon's form was sifting away. Fine black ash streamed from the figure and blew away with the wind that had come with the lightning lance. Finally all that remained was the body of a middle-aged man in golfing clothes.

Yuri nodded tiredly. That had gone as expected. Dragons were not hard to identify. And these days, slaying them was not hard either. Most of them had forgotten their true form while trying to blend into the world around them, and they could be slain before they remembered their natural powers if one was prepared, and quick enough. Yuri made a point of being prepared and quick enough.

He pulled out his cell phone, called for help, and then set to work doing CPR. It would not do to let people think he had not done all he could for the man.

A few days later he returned home. Janine had left phone messages for him, even had a gift of caviar and an invitation delivered to his office. He tried to ignore these – he needed time to think.

Yuri knew who Janine's father had been – a dragon he had killed several years before. The arrogant creature actually had lists of the offspring he had created over the years – created, and in each case, abandoned along with their mothers – both human and draconic. It was a typical pattern for dragons. The list had proved quite valuable for Yuri; it was a roadmap to his quarry. And of course, the fact that most of the offspring had been behaving true to form for dragons was merely confirmation of their parentage.

Janine was near the end of that list. Yuri did not know if her mother was human or dragon, but if her behavior fit, it didn't matter. Most offspring of dragons had very little humanity in them, he had discovered. When he slew them, they sifted away as dust. And dragon or half-blood, if they had spent substantial time as humans, they left a dead human form behind them.

Thinking of Janine, and the possibility that she was half human, made Yuri think of his wife.

Beautiful, graceful, intelligent, and as loving and generous as most of the dragons he had known were not – Yuri had worshiped the ground she walked on from the day he had met her. She had returned his love, and, at the risk of losing his love, told him that her father was a dragon. Her mother was human, so she was what the dragons called a half-blood. She could assume draconic form, although she was smaller than a full-blooded dragon.

She took him flying with her and both their hearts had soared along with their bodies. Each day they flew, unless the weather was stormy. "Lightning will kill a dragon immediately," she told him. "You'll never find a dragon flying in a storm unless he is tired of living." Dragons had inordinately long lives, and even as a half-blood, she would live for more years than he could imagine. On the day that they pledged their lives to each other, she had shared that gift with him.

"Half my life to you, so that we may grow old together," she told him. Yuri remembered how his heart had filled with wonder at her gift.

"I have nothing close to that to offer you," he told her.

"You have given me your love," she answered, "and that's enough."

She was a few months shy of delivering her first child when her brother came to visit.

"Father sent me to see what sort of nonsense you were up to," he began as soon as he entered their home. "I can see it is as bad as he said – you've prostituted yourself to this human."

"My mother was human," she had answered him frostily.

"There is no reason that you should perpetuate the mistake and further dilute our bloodline," her brother had said. He grabbed her and dragged her outside before Yuri could stop him. Then he had transformed abruptly to his true form and pierced the skin of Yuri's wife with one of his teeth.

"You will never forget again that you are a dragon," the creature had roared as the woman began a painful change to draconic form. "I have enchanted my tooth to make you change, and only my tooth will change you back. The brat you bear shall never be born, and I shall personally remove this human from the world!" She had roared back at him, a primal scream of rage, and rushed at him in fury.

The fight did not last long. She was smaller and far less experienced than he, and before Yuri could even comprehend what had happened, her body was lying on the ground before him, her blue scales losing their luster as they turned to ash and began to blow away. Very soon, all that remained was the human body of his beloved. Yuri rushed to her, hoping to find life's breath still in her, but she was gone.

Her brother, badly wounded in the fight, hissed at Yuri, "It's your fault she's dead. Yours! Had she not gifted you with a portion of her life, she would have been able to withstand the injuries and would still live. She would be human," and he spat out the word like an epithet, "but alive." With that, he blew a last gout of fire and incinerated her body.

And the man that Yuri was, the man that he became in that moment, turned upon the dragon with such ferocity that he took the dragon by surprise and slew him.

Bleeding from a score of wounds himself, Yuri had pried the enchanted tooth from the creature's jaw with the thought of destroying the thing that had been the downfall of his beloved. Then he thought better of it, and stored it away before crawling off to heal. He left the dragon's body to rot where it fell.

As he healed, Yuri had time to think. The fire of vengeance burned bright in his heart, and he knew that most dragons were of the same cloth as his beloved's brother and father – greedy and heartless, interfering in the affairs of humans whenever it was to their advantage, and killing them when they pleased. Yuri would be the force that removed them from the world. His life was long, and needed a new purpose.

The enchanted tooth would insure that he killed no greedy humans by mistake. He just needed a way to kill the dragons. He remembered how his beloved would never fly in storms, and smiled.

It took him years, but Yuri finally found a mage to teach him to call lightning down from the sky. Now he had his heavenly sword. Now he was ready, and he left to do battle on the dragons of the world. He sought them out – although those whose greed was for knowledge rather than riches or power were left in peace. He even befriended a few through time, and could count several scholars, a musician, some adventurers and a philanthropist among his draconic friends.

But on the others, he had no mercy. He was judge, jury and executioner. Patiently, he would gather information on his suspects, and when the time was right, he would test them with the tooth. He would then call down his lightning sword and swiftly make an end to them. If they did not revert to human form after death, another quick prick with the tooth took care of it. Strangely, Yuri was as unwilling as the dragons themselves to have them revealed to an unbelieving modern world.

Finally, Yuri stirred himself from his reverie. Something about Janine reminded him of his beloved. He needed to think some more. He sent another message to the lady telling her that he was on his way out of town again, and this time he would make sure to see her when he got back. In the meantime, he checked on the charity she claimed to donate to. Some skillful computer use and a little hacking, and he found that she was not lying. In fact, she was quite generous with her donations. Strange, and definitely not in character for who he thought she was. He could not allow his emotions to cloud him; his business was deadly.

Just how deadly that could be was made clear in San Diego.

Yuri had another dragon-candidate in sunny southern California. Another wealthy magnate whose not-so-widely known investments included Columbian drugs and arms sales to certain embattled areas. Bodies tended to turn up when there were inquiries made about the man. The man himself lived a reclusive life on a large estate in the hills behind the city. It was going to be a challenge just to get near him.

Once again, Yuri used a lucrative business proposition to try to gain admittance to the man's presence. It worked; Yuri was summoned to the estate by a messenger in a limousine. When he got there, he was wanded with a metal detector which naturally failed to pick up the tooth. Finally he was escorted by a rather large man to an enormous office where his quarry sat behind a desk that could have doubled for a banquet table, it was so large.

"Leave us," the man told his bodyguards curtly. As soon as they were out of the room, the man turned to Yuri with a shark-like smile. "So, you want to do business with me, do you? What makes you think you have anything I would want?" He paused, still staring at Yuri. "And what makes you think you have the cojones to do business with me?" He sat back in his chair, waiting.

Yuri, who had been parked in a small, low guest chair by his escort, started to put forth his business proposition. Since Yuri really did have a reputation as an astute (but not greedy) businessman, he thought his offer would get some consideration. But as he wound up his presentation, the man leaned forward in his chair and said, "What are you really here for, Mr. Farmer? What do you really want to do to me? It isn't to make a business offer, we both know that." The chair swung to and fro. "I've followed you a long, long time, and if I've followed you for a long time, Death has followed you for even longer. Far too many of my compatriots have not survived long after meeting you. And I think it's time that this stopped." He drew in a deep breath.

Yuri tried to look puzzled, but dropped his pretense when the man laughed at him. "Don't bother. I know who you are, what you do, and how you do it. Why do you think we are in a windowless chamber? You have no way to call your "heavenly sword" down on me. I, on the other hand, have a nice, large room to transform in. I will so enjoy this. My fellow dragons will reward me for this, too, rather richly I imagine. You have been a plague upon us for far too long." He looked at Yuri speculatively. "I think we will take this slowly. My people have been informed that they have the rest of the day off, so no one will hear your screams – or your pleas."

The man stood up behind the desk and stretched slowly. Then, still grinning in a shark-like manner, he stepped from behind his desk and began to change.

It had been years since Yuri had seen a dragon change of its own volition; it was far more leisurely than the change forced by the tooth. It seemed almost sensual for the man. He stretched and smiled as he changed, rolling his head around and writhing in a pleased manner. He kept growing and changing until finally a huge midnight blue dragon stood before him, its head almost brushing the ceiling of the chamber.

Yuri stepped back until he was pressed against the door. He fingered the tooth, but then left it. He had learned long ago that it would not work against a dragon who had taken its natural form of its own volition. His eyes darted around the room as the creature slowly advanced on him, its huge claws making gouges in the polished wood floor.

"Now, now, Mr. Farmer, you don't think I'm going to let you leave without a taste of your own sort of hospitality, do you?" A forearm snaked out and left a bleeding furrow on Yuri's arm. Yuri clutched at it and dove aside just as the dragon lashed out again. His mind was churning frantically. If the dragon was going to play with him first, he might have a chance.

He dodged and darted around the perimeter of the room as the dragon hit him with glancing blows. Yuri was bleeding, but he was still on his feet as he reached the desk. "Ah, ah, ah," the dragon shook its head and flattened the enormous slab of wood with one blow. "No hiding from your destiny!" Yuri leaped over the debris and kept on going. Finally he reached the door again. Then, as the dragon taunted him some more and he instinctively dodged its blows, Yuri began to work.

Normally he called lightning, electricity, from the sky. The sheer voltage was what killed a dragon. This room had no access to the sky, but it did have electrical outlets – a lot of them. He had located each one as he ran around the room. By themselves, they would be like a flea bite for the creature. But if he took all of them together, and pulled a charge through them that would fry every circuit for miles around, he might have a chance.

Yuri danced away from the dragon, only allowing it to score small hits on him now and then, as he worked. The dragon seemed quite happy to inflict little damages so that it could make him suffer longer. Still, Yuri was covered with blood and growing weak before he was ready. The final gathering required him to stand motionless for a short while. This was the dangerous part. Yuri suddenly darted forward, the tooth in his hand. While it would not transform the beast, it was naturally sharp enough to pierce the scales and should distract the creature while Yuri worked.

Yuri jabbed the tooth into the dragon's belly up to the hilt and pulled it out, dripping with blue-black dragon's blood. The dragon roared in rage, and while it did, Yuri danced back out of range and finished summoning the electricity. Lines of crackling power surged from every outlet in the room. Even the computer outlets under the destroyed desk contributed. Yuri pulled the power into a snapping, sparking blue-white lance and tossed it at the dragon's heart. Then he held it there, pulling more and more electricity from the wires until the room went dark.

He felt the thud as the dragon fell in the pitch black room. Yuri knew that while the dragon might be down, there was no guarantee that it was dead. He needed to finish the job as quickly as possible, but first he needed to be able to see. He fished his cellphone out of his pocket. Miraculously, it was still working after the fight. He pushed on the flashlight app and looked at the dragon. It seemed to be gone, but since it was not yet reduced to dust, he doubted it. He took the tooth and spent a nasty hour using it to remove the dragon's head. Only then did it turn to a dust that swirled around the room. This time there wasn't even a body left. The man had clearly spent a great deal of time in dragon form.

Hours later, Yuri was back at his motel, calling people and making a fuss about how the man had refused to see him. Since the dragon had planned to kill Yuri, he doubted that anyone knew he had been there, but he wanted to make sure that he would not be connected with the disappearance. The blood splatters he had left behind might be a problem, but that worry left him when he woke up to the news that the mansion had been consumed in a fire overnight. He thanked whatever had sparked the blaze – perhaps some damaged wiring from the electricity he had summoned. When the man's less savory business dealings came out (and Yuri would make sure they did), the whole thing would be blamed on his criminal associations.

Yuri didn't go straight home. He needed time to heal and think. This was the first time in years that he had been caught out and almost killed. He wondered who (or what) else knew his identity, and how he could protect himself. Perhaps it was time to disappear for a while. Dragons lived a long time, but so did he, and his life would be longer still if they didn't kill him.

After several months, Yuri finally returned to the city. He had sent messages to Janine – just enough to let her know he was thinking about her. And he was.

He thought about her charm, her laughter, her smile. He realized too, that she reminded him in several small ways of his long-dead wife. He smiled, remembering the love of his youth all those centuries ago.

Yuri continued to research Janine. He found, to his surprise, that while she certainly had draconic tendencies in the work place, she seemed to be a secret philanthropist. She may have pushed some people aside on her way up the ladder, but those she had stepped on seemed to turn up again in good positions elsewhere. It was almost as if she was trying to project an image of ruthlessness to hide a decent heart. A decent heart didn't usually go far in business, especially in a woman. If she were seen as weak, she would be destroyed quickly in the world she worked in.

He sighed. He could not allow sentimentality to get in the way of his mission. She was the daughter of a dragon, and she was showing all the outward signs of draconic greed. The altruism must be a sham.

When he got back to the city he called Janine and set up a date.

This time they had dinner at her house by the lake. She was a marvelous cook, and she had made the meal herself. To his surprise, there were no servants hovering. He said as much, and she laughed. "No, here is where I can be me. I like to do things for myself." She shrugged.

"I would have thought that someone with your reputation for ambition would require all of the trappings of wealth and position," Yuri remarked.

She leaned her head to one side, thinking. "Sometimes I think there are two of me – the woman of business and then the person who lives here, in the house by the lake." She paused. "When I'm being the person I am here, I try not to let myself think about the things the business me does. I don't think that me would be very proud." She shook herself distastefully, like a cat that has gotten caught in the rain. "So, let's not talk about her. Let's go for a walk instead." She smiled, and the smile was amazingly sweet. Yuri's heart stuttered. He saw echoes of his beloved in that smile. He steeled himself again. He could not let these reminders of his past sway him.

The evening was, as he had originally hoped, overcast with thunder in the distance. The wind ruffled the lake in short, angry bursts as they wandered down to the shore. Yuri picked up a rock and hurled it into the lake. He threw another, even harder. He was not at ease with what he was about to do.

But, he reminded himself, if she was not a dragon, she would not change when the tooth drew her blood. He knew she was a dragon. She was in business. She was behaving draconically. He should stop her before she became like the dragon in San Diego. It was his duty, his purpose in life. Her resemblance to his lost beloved must not distract him. In fact, it might even be a ploy to get close enough to him to torture and kill him, just like in San Diego. He had to stop her now.

Yuri didn't just want to jab her openly with the tooth. He didn't know why; perhaps some part of him was hoping that she wouldn't turn out to be a dragon. He needed to do it in a way that disguised the fact that he was pricking her. He remembered seeing some wild roses, and just as she started to ask him what was wrong, he turned to her with a smile. "I'll be right back," Yuri said, and ran to gather some of the fragrant pink blooms. As he came back with the roses in hand, she asked him, "By the way, you never did tell me why you called yourself Dragon in the restaurant." She giggled charmingly. "Are you a dragon?"

As she asked, she reached for the roses with a look of delight. And as she took them, he slipped the tip of the tooth that he had hidden under them into her finger to make her think it was a thorn pricking her.

"Oh!" she said, and "Ouch." And then the flowers dropped from her hands as she drew a gasping breath and the blood oozing from her fingertip thickened and turned a pearlescent white.

Sadly, he answered her question. "No, my dear, I'm not a dragon. You are."

Yuri's heart dropped as he watched her begin to change. He had known, really, in his heart of hearts, that this would happen. The woman who had manipulated lives and careers was the real Janine, not the one who cooked and contributed to charities. That, no doubt, was just a front for the world.

He flung the tooth down into the sand and raised his hands to the skies, tears streaming down his face.

"What? What is this? What is happening?" she roared. Wings flapped desperately in fear, and she flung herself around, her tail almost knocking Yuri off his feet. This was not normal – every other dragon he had changed had remembered itself immediately upon returning to its natural form. He watched, fascinated, as she finished her change. She was beautiful – a glowing white, like the color she loved to wear. He stepped towards her once more, opening his mouth to call to her. Maybe she could be saved.

Then she laughed - a terrible sound. "A dragon. Yes, I am. Interesting. I think I like this." She turned on him and began to stalk him like a cat stalking a mouse. "You are an interesting little man, Yuri Farmer. My other form – that weak and useless one – seems to be inordinately fond of you. I am too, but I think I'll like you even better as a meal. Can't let sentimentality get in the way of getting ahead, now can I? And I can tell that you'll definitely be a bit of a stumbling block. She loves you, and you know what I am."

Yuri could put it off no longer. He shouted out his command and the lance of light streaked down from the heavens. As it pierced her scales and entered her heart, she screamed. Yuri screamed too, a primal sound of anguish that he had not uttered since that dark day when his wife was murdered. The slight flame of hope for another love that he had fanned was extinguished with the life of the dragon that had been Janine.

He sat on the beach and watched the fine white ash blow the dragon's form away from Janine's body. He sobbed like a small child the entire time, and when he finally went over to the lifeless form on the sand, he could barely see for the tears. He reached out to touch her one last time while her body was still warm and he could remember her life.

And she stirred. She moaned and took a shuddering breath. Yuri froze, his mouth open. One of his tears dripped down his face and landed on her cheek, and she swiped at it irritably.

She opened her eyes, and said, "What happened? Did I just get hit by lightning?"

Yuri reached out and hauled her to him, holding her as close as he could. She had survived. She was a half-dragon, just as his wife had been, but unlike his wife, she had not given away a portion of her long life. And she had too much humanity in her to die completely when her dragon form was destroyed. No wonder full dragons hated half-bloods so. They had an extra chance at life.

Yuri clung to Janine, laughing with a joy he had all but forgotten. He could love her, just as he was longing to. He knew that with the draconic part of her burned away by the lightning sword, she would be the noble and humane woman he had found and fallen in love with. All of his centuries of loneliness were over.

"Yuri? What happened?" Janine repeated. "I had the strangest dream…"

Yuri picked her up to take her back to the house, trying to think of how to explain it all to her as he took her back to begin their lives together.

SPINNING

"So when is that spinning wheel you bought on online supposed to be here?" Tanya asked, stretching one long, tanned leg into the air to rub sunscreen on it. Kelly and Tanya were lounging by the pool at their singles apartment complex. "I can't imagine why you bought the thing; spinning – the old fashioned kind – is so….boring." Tanya engaged in the modern version of spinning, which consisted of sitting on an exercise bike and getting hot and sweaty.

Kelly considered this far more boring than turning fleece into yarn, and said so. "And it's supposed to be here any day now," she added. "The seller called me when it shipped."

Tanya gave a fake shudder and then flipped over on the chaise lounge. "Do my back, would you? I don't want to show up all sunburned for Craig tomorrow at MY spinning class. At least my version of spinning has yummy men in it."

Kelly shook her head and smiled, but she didn't say anything. She and Tanya had been friends most of their lives, and she knew that nothing would change Tanya's mind. Her thoughts went to men, tanning, and shopping, and not always in that order. And Tanya had been the one to actually find the wheel listed in the first place, hunting on websites for bargains; Tanya loved to shop. No matter what she thought of Kelly's hobbies, Tanya was a true friend and supported her.

The crate with the wheel showed up the next day while Kelly was at work. The apartment's handyman had hauled it up to her apartment and left it there in the middle of the floor. He had also left a crowbar with a note on it saying to return it to the basement when she was done.

Kelly made herself cook and eat dinner and then clean up before she took the crowbar to open the crate. Just as she pried the first board off, the doorbell rang.

Tanya was at the door, and she jumped and squealed like the crate contained a present for her. Kelly laughed. "I thought you considered it boring!" she said.

"I do, but I love opening boxes!" Tanya replied, and immediately set to helping get the crate open.

The spinning wheel was buried in all sorts of packing material. "Boy, you'd think this thing was worth the earth, not just what you paid for it," Tanya joked.

Kelly had to agree. A wooden crate, foam peanuts and huge Styrofoam braces - what on earth was so special about one antique wheel? She was glad the shipper had been careful, but this was ridiculous.

Finally they managed to get to the spinning wheel itself and pulled it out of the crate. It was a lovely old Saxony type wheel – the sort you saw in old pictures. The wheel itself was off to one side, and the parts that actually did the spinning and held the bobbin for the finished yarn were beside it. It had a single foot treadle on it. It was quite different looking from the modern castle-style wheel Kelly already owned, with a double treadle, wheel on the bottom and spinning parts and bobbin on the top. It wasn't nearly as portable either.

Not that she'd want to take this old beauty out and about. It was clearly quite old, but the wheel was in excellent condition and the workmanship was exquisite, with delicate carving on the dark wood of the legs, the sides of the wheel and pretty much anywhere that there could be carving.

Both women stood there admiring it.

"Wow. This is incredible," Kelly said. "And I got it for only $200? I paid three times that for my new wheel. Maybe it doesn't spin well or something."

"Even I can see how incredible it looks, so if it doesn't spin well, you still have a great decorating piece," Tanya said, poking around in the packing material. "Ah, here we go. I thought I saw another package."

Kelly opened the smaller box that had been in the crate. It was full of bobbins, a spare drive band and another, cloth-wrapped item. Curious now, she unwrapped whatever it was from the layers of fine linen cloth wound around it.

"Whoa, what's that? It looks like an ice pick on steroids!" Tanya pulled back away from the dangerous looking item in Kelly's hands.

"It's a quill tip for the wheel. It's used for extra-fast, extra fine spinning, like cotton or silk," Kelly replied with a puzzled look on her face. "This wasn't listed as one of the parts."

"So they forgot to list it. It's not like they didn't send you something that was listed."

"Good point. Well, help me get this stuff out of the way and I'll set it up and give it a test-spin, so to speak. You can watch," Kelly added, glancing at Tanya out of the corner of her eye with an amused expression. Tanya always ran for the hills when Kelly sat down to spin or knit, saying that if she wanted to be bored, she'd watch paint dry.

But to her surprise, Tanya twitched a little, almost made a face, and then smiled brightly and said, "Sure."

This was not in character, but Kelly was too interested in trying out the new wheel to pursue it right now. She filed it away for later action, nodded, and started wrestling the crate and packing material to the door with the dubious help of Kelly's two cats, who thought that the Styrofoam peanuts and other packing material had been delivered just for them to play with. Kelly finally got the worst of the packing stuff inside and shoved the crate out the door; the maintenance man would pick it up later.

The room was cleared, the wheel was moved to the side of the room where Kelly kept her spinning things, and thoroughly dusted and oiled. Kelly checked the tension, set up the bobbin with a fresh leader, and took out some soft grey wool that was ready to spin. Her foot pumped the treadle, and the wheel started to turn. Moments later the grey wool was flowing through her fingers quickly. "It's like butter," she breathed, reaching for another piece of the grey fiber.

When she stopped to move the yarn so the bobbin would fill evenly, she looked over at Tanya with stars in her eyes. "This was only $200? It spins as well as the high-end wheels I've tried out. And let me tell you, they cost WAY more than $200. More like two thousand."

"You look like you just found Prince Charming. Well, you know it wasn't a mistake – you paid with PayPal and the seller accepted it."

"Yeah, I know. But I just keep thinking that there has to be a catch." She shook her head in disbelief and reached for another piece of fiber to spin.

"Speaking of Prince Charming - how is Craig? That's his name, right? Mr. Hunk-o-Beefcake from your exercise class?"

"Never mind. Let's just say that good looks can hide a serious jerk."

"Ah." That was all Kelly said, but she was thinking, "Well, that explains why she's so eager to hang out here tonight. I'm a handy excuse." Not that this bothered her. After all, what were girlfriends for? And she really did enjoy the company.

Tanya stayed for the entire evening, finally leaving when they were both yawning too much to talk anymore and Kelly had a bobbin full of soft grey yarn and another half full of red. "Come by tomorrow and watch me finish the red and then ply it with the grey for some sock yarn for my dad," she joked. She was shocked when Tanya readily agreed.

Kelly went to bed thoughtful. This guy must be really bad if Tanya wanted to hang out and watch her spin again. Yes, they were talking and having fun too, but Tanya never wanted to do that two nights in a row – there were always guys to go out with and parties to go to. It was almost like she was hiding.

Tanya did indeed show up the next night, bearing wine, cheese and a good movie. The evening was peaceful, and Tanya even commented on the finished yarn. "Looks like some old boot socks I used to have." She paused, "Do you mind if I stay the night?"

"Sure you can," Kelly replied. She looked at Tanya quizzically. Tanya rarely wanted to stay; she said Kelly's place was too quiet for her tastes. "But, really? You've refused the last three times I invited you."

Tanya paused for a moment. "Oh, the air conditioner in my apartment is acting up. I called the handyman, but he hasn't fixed it yet. You know how it is." She shrugged one shoulder.

Kelly did. For a so-called luxury singles apartment complex, it was pretty lousy – cheaply made, poor service and rent that increased with every lease renewal. "Yeah. Score another one for Tuckertown Enterprises. Well, you know where the spare room is. Have at! I'm pooped and I'm going to bed." As Kelly headed for her bedroom, she could hear Tanya checking the bolt on the door.

The next night was Friday night, and Kelly spent it peacefully by herself. She finished spinning the yarn she had started the night before and then took out the quill tip. She wanted to start experimenting with it on Saturday, so she spent the rest of the evening looking up on-line videos on how to use the thing. She didn't hear from Tanya at all, which didn't surprise her, since Kelly knew that Tanya always went out with a pack of girlfriends who shared her love of crowds and noise on Fridays.

However, when Tanya called at noon on Saturday and asked her to go to lunch at a rather pricey restaurant, Kelly was a bit surprised.

First, noon was the crack of dawn for Tanya on Saturdays. Second, it was the end of the month and Tanya was usually too broke for nice restaurants by the end of the month.

Kelly put her spinning wheel in the corner by the chair her cats claimed as their own. It was far enough out of the way that hopefully no one should get jabbed on the pointy end of the quill tip.

The idea proved to be less than satisfactory. Sheba, the female grey tiger, loved to rub against wool and clearly thought that the wheel being right by her chair was the best invitation she had had in ages. She meowed, chirped, and then rubbed her cheek ecstatically against the yarn wound at the base of the quill. She squinted her eyes shut and then ramped it up a notch by standing on the arm of the chair and rubbing the entire length of her body down the quill, stropping back and forth.

Kelly snorted with annoyance and went to move the wheel. She didn't mind Sheba rubbing a little, but at this rate, the yarn would be more cat hair than wool. She grabbed the wheel to move it just as Sheba was finishing a pass. The quill tip glanced off Sheba's flirting tail as Kelly pulled the wheel away and Sheba squeaked with annoyance, promptly sitting down to lick at the injured appendage.

"Cry-baby," Kelly told her. "You're not hurt. Look, no blood." She rubbed the cat's striped tail as she spoke.

Sheba was not impressed, and flipped her tail derisively before she turned her back on Kelly and ostentatiously curled into a ball for a nap. Kelly rolled her eyes at the theatrics and moved the wheel to the opposite corner. It was not quite as out of the way there, but at least it wouldn't be covered in Sheba hairs.

Tanya was already waiting when Kelly got to the restaurant. She was in a dark booth at the back of the place, wearing sunglasses, a hat, and looking around nervously from behind her menu.

"You look like an actress in a bad spy movie." Kelly slid into the booth.

"Shhh. Keep your voice down, for crying out loud," Tanya hissed.

"What on earth are you doing, Tanya? What is going on?"

Tanya glanced around cautiously before she answered. "You know that guy, Craig? The hot one from my spinning class?"

Kelly nodded. "I'm trying to avoid him. I know he hates the food in this place, so I thought it would be a good place for lunch."

"What's wrong with just eating at home?"

"He knows where I live, stupid. I think he knows where you live, too, since he lives in the complex with us. I stayed at Cassie's last night. He doesn't know her, so I figured I'd be safe there."

"Wait a second, Tanya – are you saying you're afraid of this guy? He's some kind of stalker or something?"

"Or something. He started to get really weird the last time we went out, and that night after I went home, I could have sworn I heard somebody playing with the lock on my door. I got the maintenance guy to change the lock the next day, but I haven't stayed there since."

"Have you seen this Craig around still?"

"Yeah, I have. A couple of times. He keeps popping up in places that I go to a lot. I know, I know," she nodded, "it could be a coincidence, since we like the same sorts of things, but he's always alone and he's always looking at me. And I think I've seen him other places, like by my work, but I'm not sure." She made a face and shrugged. "And maybe I'm just paranoid. Maybe my party-hardy lifestyle is taking the toll mother always said it would." She lapsed into a depressed silence.

"First of all, your lifestyle shouldn't be making you paranoid – your mom always was full of baloney. Second, if you thing you're seeing him, you may be. What did he do on that last date that creeped you out so much?"

"He was way beyond gropey. He was really pushing me to, well, you know, but I wasn't ready to. I mean, I've gone out with pushy guys before, and guys who think I should put out just because they bought me dinner, but he was verging on violent. He was talking to me like I was a street-walker he'd paid for, and he was really starting to get physical with me. Then the phone rang, and while I answered it, he left. This guy is really, really bad news."

"Did he hurt you?"

Tanya showed Kelly her arm and the bruise on it.

"Did you call the cops?"

"Yeah. They said I could swear out a restraining order against him, but that was about it. The bruise hadn't shown up yet, and it's the kind of shape that could be from anything."

"Crap," said Kelly.

"Yeah, that and a whole lot worse," replied Tanya.

"Well, the first thing we have to do is make sure you're safe."

"Got that taken care of. I'm taking some vacation and going home to stay with Mom for a few days, until it looks like this thing has blown over. That's what I wanted to talk to you about today. I don't want to go back to my apartment for anything. Can you go and pick up a few things for me later today? And mail them to my mom's?" She produced a list from her purse.

"Sure, you know I can. Are you sure that's all I can do?"

"Yeah, for now. Hey, I'll call, stay in touch, you know. It shouldn't be for long. He should lose interest pretty quickly if I'm not around."

Kelly wasn't so sure, but she kept silent about it. They ordered lunch, and afterward Tanya slunk away, once again reminding Kelly of a bad spy movie.

Kelly went straight to Tanya's apartment. It was in another wing of the apartment complex – a fancier one than Kelly's, with a tiny balcony patio, upgraded appliances and a Jacuzzi tub that occasionally worked. Kelly lived in the wing reserved for pet owners, where for a moderately huge deposit (which you were guaranteed never to get back), you could have one small dog or two cats. No large dogs, no extra pets, no birds larger than a budgie.

The door was locked, but it looked like someone other than Tanya had been there. There wasn't anything she could put her finger on, just things not quite where Tanya would leave them, that sort of thing. She quickly collected the things that Tanya wanted and put them all in a big straw bag that Tanya used when they went to the lake.

She was locking the door when someone came up behind her. "So, where's Tanya? And why were you in her apartment?" a deep voice asked. Really, this guy's voice conjured up movie stars it was so rich and warm. Kelly whirled and faced the speaker. His looks matched his voice. She knew immediately that this must be Craig.

She looked him up and down and, thinking on her feet and hefting the straw bag, answered coolly, "On a trip, and she forgot a few things." She stepped back and continued, "Who are you to be asking about Tanya? Seems to me that if she wanted you to know she'd have told you herself."

The man's eyes hardened and his mouth tightened. "Who the hell are you, her keeper?" he snarled. He was reaching for her when one of the doors down the hall opened, and he snatched his hands back. "Tell her that Craig is looking for her, would you?" he finished in the voice she had first heard. The change had been like lightning, and a smile that did not reach his eyes lifted his lips.

Kelly smiled sweetly, "Of course I will." She slipped away before he had another chance to reach for her, and as soon as she was out of sight, she ran like the wind for the safety of her own apartment.

Kelly slammed her door and slid all of the bolts home. "Crap!" she said to the cat that came to meet her, her orange striped male Gopher (he liked to burrow in the blankets). "That dude is even nastier than Tanya said. And now I really don't think a few weeks with her mom are going to be enough."

Putting the bag down by the door, she went to find a box to mail the things in. Gopher wound around her ankles, almost tripping her, until she said, "All right, I give in, I'll feed you first."

As she was opening the cans of cat food in the kitchen, she noticed that Gopher was still the only cat dancing attendance on her. Odd, but not terribly so. Sheba was probably still mad at her, and was hiding somewhere. She did that occasionally. The can of cat food was already open. Kelly looked at it, sighed, and put it down anyway. Sheba would no doubt turn up to eat it as soon as Kelly, the object of her feline ire, left.

Kelly found the box, packed up the things for Tanya, and headed for the post office, completely forgetting that it was Saturday afternoon and they would be closed. After some cursing and grousing, she finally ended up at one of those stores that will have packages picked up for a small fee – about an arm and a pint of blood, by Kelly's calculations. Then she had to go the store, since she was almost out of both cat and people food. All in all, it was almost dark by the time she got home.

Dumping her bags down in the kitchen, she was annoyed to find Gopher winding around her legs again.

"Dude, I know you can't be that hungry." Both food dishes were empty, which meant that either Sheba had condescended to eat or Gopher had cleaned out both bowls, but either way, Gopher should not be hungry. Finally, she removed him from the kitchen and shut him in the bedroom while she put the groceries away and made herself some dinner.

When she was ready to sit and spin and watch TV, she let him out again and they proceeded to the living room together. He immediately jumped up on the cats' chair, where Kelly was shocked to see Sheba still snoozing away, in exactly the same position she was in when Kelly left before lunch. Gopher was nosing her and meowing softly. He started grooming her gently around the ears and face.

Alarmed, Kelly rushed over to the chair. Was Sheba sick? Was this why Gopher was upset? But as she got there, Sheba stretched and yawned, reaching up to lick Gopher back in the mutual grooming they often engaged in. Still ignoring Kelly, she jumped down and sauntered off to the kitchen, where she found the dry food that Kelly left down for them to snack on. Kelly could hear her crunching from the living room.

"Blasted drama queen of a cat," she remarked to Gopher, who was now busily grooming his underside with one leg stuck up in the air. He ignored her too, so she pulled out her spinning wheel and worked with the quill tip again. She mulled over rooting through her stash for the cotton she had bought on a whim one time, but decided to leave it for the next day. It was Sunday, and she could take the whole day with her wheel and really learn how to spin the cotton. She would look forward to that.

Late that night, after she was in bed, Kelly thought she heard someone at her door. Sitting up in bed and holding very still, she didn't hear anything else. The cats were fur balls on the bed with her, and when they didn't move, she decided that Tanya's paranoia was catching, especially after meeting the slime ball today. She lay down and, after tossing restlessly for a while, went back to sleep.

Sunday was a day that Kelly reserved for her own special use – no errands, no appointments, nothing but what she wanted to do. And today, what she wanted to do was learn to spin cotton on her new wheel. She got out the cotton fiber and set up the wheel and quill tip. Referring one last time to the videos she had found, she started and slowly built up speed and confidence. When she had the shaft half-full of fiber, she stopped for lunch. And discovered that she didn't have any bread. Even after the shopping yesterday, she still didn't have bread. Well, she'd have to go out anyway today.

"Crud," she said. The cats looked at her expectantly. She was in the kitchen, after all. This might mean she was going to feed them canned food. When she grabbed her purse instead, they stalked off indignantly to the living room.

On her way to the door, Kelly put her wheel away in the corner she had used yesterday. No point in leaving it out where she could fall over it when she got home.

A quick trip to the store turned into another big shopping session as Kelly kept finding things she realized she had forgotten yesterday. She must have been more distracted by Tanya's problems than she thought. Finally, though, loaded down with bags, she unlocked the door to her apartment and pushed her way in. She left half the bags by the door and took the first batch to the kitchen. Forget needing a shopping cart at the store; she needed one to get the bags from the car to the kitchen once she got home – either that, or stop buying so much.

When she returned to get the second batch of bags, she saw him. Craig was standing there, staring at her. Once again, the smile on his face didn't reach his eyes.

"You know, you really should lock your door, even if you are coming right back," he said softly, moving towards her into the room. "I thought this was where you lived – I followed Tanya here one night." He moved like the cats did when they were stalking something, his eyes never leaving her face. Kelly was backing up into the living room eyes casting around frantically.

"Looking for this?" He held up her purse, which contained her cell phone. "Probably shouldn't have left it by the door, either."

"Wha…What do you want?" she gulped, trying to work some moisture into her suddenly parched mouth. She had backed into the middle of the living room now. If she could get to the kitchen, she could get the window open and could scream for help. That, and grab a knife from her knife holder.

But Craig seemed to know what she was thinking, because he suddenly darted forward and grabbed her arms, pinning them to her sides. Kelly kicked out at him in panic, and one shoe connected with his knee. He danced back, swearing, but didn't release his grip. She tried again, this time aiming for his crotch, but his arms were long and he kept her off balance enough that she couldn't connect.

She was screaming the whole time, but Craig just laughed. "I happen to know that the folks on either side of you and below you are out. If you think someone will hear you on the street down there, well, I guess we'll have to take that chance. As for what I want, I bet you can figure that out – you seem like a smart girl. Since Tanya isn't around, I'll take you instead. And then when Tanya comes back to bury her best friend, I'll take her too."

Seeing the horrified expression on Kelly's face, he grinned, a scary sight in that picture-perfect face. "Oh yes, I've done this before. And they haven't caught me yet – I'm very careful."

Kelly now noticed the thin vinyl gloves on his hands. She screamed again, and tried to twist loose. This time, she succeeded. She took two quick steps and grabbed a lamp off the table beside the cats' chair and flung it at him as hard as she could. It was a large, heavy ginger-jar lamp, and he had to raise his arms to protect his face from it. The impact knocked him back several steps, and the lamp landed at his feet.

"So that's the way you want to play." His face twisted in a snarl, Craig stepped forward again to grab her. Kelly wasn't watching, she was making her way back towards the front door and reaching for another lamp to stall him some more while she escaped. So whatever made him lose his balance, the lamp at his feet, one of the cats fleeing the mayhem near their chair, or simple fate, she never knew. She just knew that when she turned to fling the other lamp at him he was already reeling backwards toward the corner where her spinning wheel was stored. She flung the next lamp at him anyway and whirled to reach the front door. She heard a thud and another curse – he must have connected with the sharp point of the quill tip as the fell against the thing.

Kelly fumbled with the lock and realized that he had done something to jam it. She turned back around, her back pressed to the door, and grabbed for a bag of groceries to hurl at him.

She turned back in time to see him disentangle himself from the spinning wheel and lurch forward, towards her. Then he just stood there for a second, a bemused expression on his face, before he collapsed forward. He landed on his face on the ginger-jar lamp. The ceramic broke under the assault. He lay there, immobile as she finally got the door open. She was screaming for help as she wrenched the door open and fell into the hall.

The police came, with an ambulance. The EMT's picked Craig up to take him to the hospital as she gave the police her report. No matter what was done to him, Craig did not wake up – the consensus was that he probably had a concussion from his impact with the lamp and the floor.

The lamp had done his lovely face quite a disservice – his nose was broken, he was missing several teeth, and his face was a jigsaw puzzle of cuts. "Now his face will fit his personality," Kelly remarked to the policeman vindictively. The man smiled in agreement.

But the concussion didn't explain why he had collapsed to begin with. "Probably some drug he was on," remarked the detective. He turned to the EMT's. "Get Sleeping Beauty out of here, would you? This lady's seen enough of him for one day."

After all the pictures were taken and the police had left, leaving her with a card for a forensic cleaning company that would get Craig's potentially dangerous blood out of her carpet, Kelly looked around at the damage. Really, aside from the lamps and the carpet, there was little to show for what had almost happened in her apartment. Her spinning wheel was even still upright and in one piece; apparently it was built to last. But then her gaze fell on the quill tip with its load of newly spun cotton. It was destroyed, broken in half. Tears sprang up in her eyes. It was the last straw, and the dam broke. She was still sitting there, sobbing like a baby when Tanya came in. Tanya had been the first call after the police. Tanya sat there on the floor with her, rocking her while she cried. Finally, she wiped her eyes, hiccupped and blew her nose in the tissue Tanya offered her.

"It's not even the quill tip, really. I know it's silly to cry over something like that, that I can replace, that I didn't even expect to own a week ago."

Tanya shook her head. "You're crying over the whole thing, I know. Come on, I'll get the broom and dustpan and you take that thing apart. It looks like the wheel is okay except for that. I know a guy who does wood working. I'll bet I can get him to make you a new part, easy as that!" She hugged Kelly and left for the kitchen while Kelly took the broken part off the wheel and put it in a box for disposal.

A few weeks later, Kelly and Tanya sat at the table in Kelly's kitchen, talking. Kelly's apartment was completely back to normal and her spinning wheel sported a brand-new, custom made part from one of Tanya's many guy friends. Tanya was still staying at Kelly's apartment; Kelly couldn't stand the idea of staying alone yet.

"So, the cops said that Craig is the suspect in a string of rapes and a few murders. He was doing something they called escalating, becoming more violent every time. They have a bunch of DNA that ties him to all of those crimes." Kelly hugged herself, suddenly chilled.

Tanya felt chilled too. "When I think of what almost happened. And God, I feel so responsible…"

"Yeah, but if it hadn't been me, someone else might be dead and he might still be on the loose."

"True. Well, if he ever wakes up, they'll nail him and he'll never get out from behind bars." Then Tanya smiled. "Hey, did I ever tell you what my buddy Tony, who's a nurse at General, says they call Craig?"

Kelly shook her head.

"Sleeping Beauty, because he won't wake up and they don't know why."

"Yeah, the EMT's called him that when they were hauling him away."

"Yeah, but the kicker is how awful he looks now. His nose will never be nice again, and he has scars all over his face from the cuts. He's anything but a beauty, and they joke that if he needs a kiss from his true love to wake up, he's going to be waiting an awfully long time, because between his face and his personality, nobody's going to want to be his true love."

Both women burst into laughter, but Kelly was thoughtful for a while. That quill tip hadn't been part of the advertised package, and she remembered the reaction of Sheba after the tip poked her and the way she hadn't awakened until Gopher had "kissed" her.

Then there was the strange way Craig had collapsed after his collision with it, and the fact that he didn't wake up.

Nah, it couldn't be…things like that didn't happen in real life.

MY BIG BROTHER SAYS

The full moon filtered through the branches of the trees at the edge of the woods, its light glowing brighter as the sun finished setting. Four boys sat around in a circle, with a flashlight in the center of the group. Two small tents were set up a short way back.

"...And when they got back to the house, the guy goes around to open the girl's car door and there's this hook hanging off of it!" one of the boys finished with a flourish.

"Yeah, yeah, we've all heard that one before..."

"No! I swear it happened to a friend of my big brother's! He told me so himself!" defended the first boy.

"Yeah, well, my big brother went into this haunted house, see, and...."

One of the boys shifted slightly and looked at his watch and then at the full moon overhead, and finally at the western horizon, where the last grey light of dusk still hung.

He turned to the group as the third boy finished his tale, and all the boys groaned.

"Do you really believe that, man?"

"Your brother is such a dork!"

"Yeah, he's so full of it!"

The ghost story telling quickly degenerated into whose big brother was the biggest pain. Three of the boys were ready to go on at length on this topic.

Finally, as full dark arrived, the fourth boy finally spoke up.

"My big brother says that these woods have monsters in them."

"Monsters?!"

"Yeah, right!"

"And you believe him? Come on, man!"

"Yeah, I believe him. I think he's right. There are monsters here."

"Then why'd you come camping with us, huh?"

"Yeah, why?"

"Aw, he's just trying to scare us! There aren't any monsters here. Either that or he's trying to prove that his big brother is the worst!"

The other boys all burst out laughing. "Anyway," one of them added, "we're right in his backyard, or almost. You can see the lights of his house from here!"

The fourth boy waited until they were done, and said, "That's why I'm here. I knew you wouldn't believe me, so I came along, especially since you were going to be camping in the state forest right by my house. This way, maybe I can help you get away from the monster."

"Yeah, right. So maybe you and your brother can work something up to scare us all!"

"Oooohhhh!" the other boys joined in.

Then one of the other boys spoke up. "No, his brother is going to be out of town. I heard his mom talking to my mom yesterday, when they were talking about us camping out. She said that he wouldn't be available to come camping with us because he wanted to go to visit his uncle or something."

The fourth boy twitched nervously and looked at the moon again. "He says that there are monsters here for sure and they like to come out on nights like tonight. He says I shouldn't come out here on nights like tonight."

"Yeah, well, your mom and dad didn't have a problem! I think he's just trying to scare you and us, too!"

The fourth boy shrugged, "They don't know. They've never seen it, and they don't go out at night anyway."

"So how does your brother know?"

"He's seen it. More than once, too."

"No way, man!"

"Serious?"

"Yeah. And, well, I have too. Sorta. I've seen something, anyway. Eyes, you know, and something running through the underbrush."

"And you came anyway. Even though you say you know there's a monster here."

The other boys were still acting derisive but they were on the verge of believing, the fourth boy knew. He needed to hurry though, because time was running out.

"I came because I knew I could convince you if I was here, and we could all get away safe."

There was a rustling in the underbrush near the edge of the tiny camp.

The fourth boy looked over quickly and was visibly relieved when a bird flew up.

The other boys shifted uneasily.

"Man, you're scaring me."

"Yeah, me too."

The third boy gulped nervously but didn't say anything. He looked around at the dark woods.

The fourth boy said, "We should leave now. It'll only take us a few minutes to get back to my house, and we'll be safe there. My folks won't care if we spend the night in the basement rec room."

There were more noises from the bushes nearby. These were louder, as if something big were moving around.

No one said anything.

Something that sounded like a growl came from the distance.

The boys looked around, frightened.

One of them gasped and pointed, "Eyes, big red eyes, over there!"

This time the growl was clear, low and menacing.

"RUN!" shouted the fourth boy.

The three boys ran shrieking for the house several hundred yards away. The fourth boy got to his feet but stood his ground.

As something large and hairy, with glowing red eyes and fearsome, dripping fangs emerged into the clearing, growling, the boy reached into his pocket and spoke, "You know, I almost didn't get them out of here in time! You really need to do something about this, you know! Just think how you'd feel if you actually ate someone!" Then he pulled a small package from his pocket and threw the contents in the face of the advancing creature.

As the powdered wolfsbane and silver mixture flew into its eyes and nose, the werewolf took off running into the woods. The boy shook his head and sighed. "And they think their big brothers are a pain in the butt!" Then he let out a convincing shriek and ran for the house to join the others.

THE FORGOTTEN PATH

Tim stood in the rough clearing. It was nearly dark, and the wind was rising. Behind him he could hear his mother's quiet, desperate sobs and the whimpers of fear from his younger sister. He could feel his life teetering on the cusp of change, tilting to plummet over the edge of familiarity into something far stranger than he could ever have imagined yesterday.

That morning – the morning of his twenty-first birthday – had begun ordinarily enough. Tim had risen when his alarm went off at six, dressed in his dark suit and tie and readied himself to go off to another day's work as a junior accountant at a large firm in the city. He planned to lunch with co-workers and then go out to celebrate his twenty-first birthday at various clubs and bars with his friends. He would finally be part of their crowd; finishing college early had made him the youngest in his office and the odd man out for social gatherings. Now perhaps he could fit in.

Tim had never really fit in, despite his and, when he was younger, his mother's best efforts. They had come to the city when he was seven, right after his sister was born. Tim vaguely remembered a life somewhere rural before that time, but the memories were fuzzy. Still, he had never been entirely comfortable in the vast concrete jungle that his mother and sister loved.

His mother had done her best to help him fit in. He had ridden public transportation, played ball in the street in front of his apartment house, gone swimming at the Y and generally lived a city boy's life. His mother insisted that he do well in school, and he had, graduating from high school a year younger than his classmates and then completing the accounting degree his mother wanted him to get in three years.

He had always begged to spend time in the park where things grew outside of boxes, but his mother merely shook her head, shuddered and then said too quickly, "Muggers. There are muggers at the park." So he went with her to museums or shopping instead and snuck away to the green places and hung out there without her knowing, the way other young people snuck away to the bars or hung out on street corners. He thought sadly sometimes that she would have been happier if he had been on the street corners, had she known where he was.

So Tim, being a person who liked to please, fell into the life that his mother wanted for him and his sister seemed to love, and lived life as a city boy and then a city man. It always felt artificial for him, and he had to try too hard at it, and it never really worked.

Tim had awakened that morning with hazy memories of dreams of another time and place. He had the odd feeling that they were real memories from the time before he moved to the city, but he wasn't sure. The dreams hung over him and left him foggy-headed. A cold shower did nothing to wake him up, and he decided that there wasn't enough coffee in the world to clear his head.

His mother called to wish him a happy birthday as he sat eating his breakfast. He accepted her good wishes, and his sister's, with a smile and then asked, "Mother, where was it that we lived before we moved here? I was thinking about it and I just can't remember."

He didn't think he imagined the hesitation in her voice when she answered, "On the old farm that my grandparents had. Why?"

"Just curious," he replied. He knew better than to push her; she would just clam up the way she always had when he had asked about life before the city. "Listen, I better get going. And don't call me early tomorrow morning – I'm going out with the gang tonight to celebrate the big two-one. We've got some major clubbing planned!" he finished brightly. But already his mind was racing. The old farm. He remembered now. It was about a hundred miles away. He could get there by mid-morning if he left now.

Tim called work to let them know that he was taking the day off after all and then grabbed his car keys. A ten-minute walk to the parking garage where he kept his clunker of a car, and then he was navigating the crowded city streets toward the open road.

Lunchtime found him in a small town asking directions to the old Sutter place. The fellow at the gas station looked at him curiously, but told him how to find it. "Ain't nobody lived there for about fifteen years or so," he said.

"Fourteen. It's been fourteen years exactly," Tim replied half under his breath. The man stared at him as he drove off.

The old place was down at the end of several long rutted dirt roads. When Tim turned the final corner and saw the burned-out hulk of the original farmhouse, his heart skipped a beat. He remembered seeing that all the time when he was younger. How could he have forgotten how it looked, with the vines and creepers covering the stone foundation and chimney? He paused a moment and looked at it, then followed the faint ruts around the ruins and past the fallen-in barn, through the woods to the little log house that had been built generations before. His grandparents had lived there after the big house burned, and he had lived there with his mother until the day of his seventh birthday.

He remembered the way there. Even though he had not remembered it in years, he thought he could have found the way in the dark, in a storm. Each turn of the almost non-existent road was familiar, and it took his breath away, his heart pumping with excitement. He didn't know where the anticipation came from, but it was boiling up from his heart and leaving him trembling.

When he finally rolled up in front of the log house, he sat in his car for a few minutes, just remembering. He remembered coming home with his mother and a car full of groceries and library books, his mother laughing in a way she had not laughed since, unforced and relaxed and bubbling with pleasure. He remembered her sitting on the little porch with a cup of tea as he played in the yard. He remembered helping her with the vegetable garden that had been in the back. He could recall details that astounded him; things he had been trying unsuccessfully to remember for years.

When he got out of the car and walked towards the house, other memories surfaced. He remembered the bunny he had kept in a hutch around the side of the house one year. He remembered watching a robin raise her young in the apple tree by the side of the house. He remembered his mother laying a blanket on the grass on summer nights and showing him the stars, teaching him their names.

As his feet thumped on the weathered wooden steps, Tim realized that the house was in amazingly good repair. The yard looked mowed, although droppings indicated that the lawn mower was actually deer. But there were no broken windows, and everything on the porch – the rocking chairs, the little table – all looked like he and his mother had left just yesterday.

Tim stared at the door for a moment, and then reached up above it and took down the spare key he remembered his mother always kept on the ledge. It was strange. Yesterday he couldn't remember any of this, and today the memories were pouring into his head like water through a broken dam.

The door creaked open and Tim stepped through into another time. Except for a thick layer of dust, the room was completely unchanged from the day they had left. His mother's knitting sat in a basket by her rocker in front of the fireplace. His blocks, that he had been playing with the morning of their departure, still made a castle on the hearth rug. To one side, the dining table held a vase with the dust of decayed flowers surrounding it. There was firewood stacked by the fireplace, and a pile of library books on a shelf by the door. Tim picked one up, paging through it idly. *The Boxcar Children* – he had been reading his way through that series, he remembered now. They had left so quickly that his mother hadn't even returned the library books.

Tim wandered through the kitchen, where ancient cans rusted or bulged on the shelves and old food packages wore layers of dust so thick he couldn't see what they had held. Oddly, there were no mouse leavings or chewed and shredded cardboard. Tim slipped into the bathroom, remembering playing with his boats in the giant claw-footed tub. Their toothbrushes still hung over the sink. He stepped into his mother's room, with the lilacs peeping in the back window. Her hair brush lay on the dresser, and there were clothes in the closet and shoes under the edge of the bed. There was a bassinet in the corner waiting for the baby his mother had been big with, and the little clothes all tucked in a small dresser beside it.

Then Tim went up the steep, narrow stairs to the little room under the eaves that had been his.

It was just as he remembered it. His bed lay beside the window at the end of the room. He had always looked out the window as he fell asleep, he remembered, watching the snow fall or the rain drip or the wind blow. He had watched the moon and the stars as they wheeled in the night sky. And there was something else. He could almost remember, but not quite – it seemed like he had waited to see something each night. It felt like it must be important, but he just couldn't remember what it was.

He walked over to his bed, ducking slightly with the low, sloping ceiling. His bed was covered with the quilt his mother made him when he was five. It was deep blue with stars all over it; he could still see them under the dust. She had told him that this way he could sleep under the stars no matter what the weather was outside. He had giggled about that as he snuggled under it each night.

And there on the pillow was Bippo-the-Hippo, stuffed sides worn smooth from a small boy's loving. He reached out and touched the toy, his fingers clutching it convulsively as he recalled crying for its comfort after they left for the city.

"I'll get you another one. There are wonderful toy stores in the city," his mother had said. And she had been true to her word, but the newer toys hadn't been the same. Still, he had tried to please his mother and only cried for his stuffed companion at night when she couldn't see.

The rest of the room brought back more memories. The rag rug his mother had made on winter evenings, the shelf of beloved picture books, the cars and trains on the toy shelf. His collection of rocks, snail shells, nuts and leaves that had turned to dusty piles. And in the dresser and closet he found the clothing left behind that day. His jeans, t-shirts, sweaters and flannel shirts. There were little socks and boots and a felted jacket that he remembered wearing in the woods on chilly days.

The woods. Tim turned back to the window in a rush and looked.

Yes, there it was. The path. It was almost gone, nothing more than a narrow crack between the trees. You had to know exactly where to look, or you would never find it. He had forgotten all about the path and the woods.

They had been in the woods the day they left. They had been in the woods every day, for that matter. Tim had known every tree and flower and creature in there by the time he turned seven. He remembered that now. But something had happened that day, and he needed to know what it was. There was someone else in his memory, too - if he could just remember who.

Tim hurried down the stairs, hitting his head on the ceiling on the way down, and raced out the back door towards the path. He heard something as he crossed the yard; it sounded like a car door. And then, just before he slipped in between the trees, he heard his mother's voice.

"Tim! Wait! Don't!"

He turned to see her racing towards him, his fourteen-year-old sister Rosy trailing after her, looking confused.

"Tim, I knew, somehow I knew…Let's go home and talk about this. I've been afraid…Let's just go!" his mother said, clearly very agitated.

Tim shook his head. "I knew something about the move to the city was odd. I had forgotten so much. But now when I see how we literally left everything – Mom, I need to know what happened. And I know, somehow, that it has something to do with this path and the woods. I'm an adult now, and I need to remember. I'm going in. You can follow me or not, as you wish. But you aren't stopping me." With that, he stepped into the green light of the woods.

Tim took his time as he started down the path. He remembered bits and pieces – his mother showing him the plants and teaching him their names. Climbing a tree and trying to see if he could sit still enough for the birds to perch beside him. Wading in a little stream and trying to catch the water bugs that scooted on its surface.

As he walked deeper and deeper into the forest, he thought he saw a face here and there in the leaves and in the bark of the trees. It was always the same face, male, and it seemed familiar to him somehow. He shook his head. The mind played tricks like that, he knew. There was even a scientific name for it - matrixing.

Finally, Tim stepped into a small clearing. It was here, he remembered, that they had been right before his mother had fled the woods and dragged him off to the city. Sitting in the center of the area, he closed his eyes and tried to remember what had happened.

Slowly, the memory returned. He had been playing with her, and with someone else, but he couldn't remember who. It was sprinkling rain, but the day was warm and no one was concerned about it. He had been laughing as he dodged the raindrops, and then he had joked that he would like to make it rain leaves instead. He had swept his hand through the air, and leaves – a whole tree full of them, had appeared and rained down on them. He had stopped, his mouth open with amazement.

The other person with them – a man, Tim recalled now, had laughed too, and told him that since his mother liked lilacs so, perhaps he should make it rain lilacs for her. Tim had grinned and swung his arm towards his mother and the air had been filled with fragrant lilac blooms floating down around his mother. His mother had stopped laughing and playing, her eyes wide and frightened. The man – his face was so very familiar - had looked at Tim with pride and said….he had said, "On your seventh birthday, too. I am proud of you, my son."

Son. The man was his father. Now Tim thought back again, and he realized that it had been this man – his father – who had taught him the names of the plants, and how to sit still enough to charm the birds. He had spent each and every day of his young life in the woods with this man and yet, somehow, until this moment he had forgotten it. He had no memories of the man in the cabin, just in the woods.

Agitated, Tim jumped to his feet and began to pace around the clearing to see what else he could remember. As he did so, he heard footsteps on the path he had followed in and turned to see his mother and sister entering the clearing. His mother looked strangely at home in the woods, even though she was clearly upset. His sister, the city child, looked frazzled and dirty and very unhappy.

Tim heard footsteps behind him and turned again. Standing before him was the man of his memories.

"Timothy." And in the man's pronunciation of his name, Tim saw waving fields of golden hay, plants fragrant in the summer sun.

"Father?" Tim replied, and the man grinned at him, a slightly feral gesture that Tim remembered seeing many times before.

"Tim, don't!" his mother cried behind him.

The man looked beyond Tim at the woman, sorrow in his gaze. "Did you really think that by taking him away you could change things?" he asked gently. "Nature is what it is."

Tim turned slightly so that he could see both of his parents at once. "Why did you take me, Mother? Why did we go? I remember – I think I remember, anyway – something about leaves and lilacs. You got upset and dragged me down the path." Tim paused, remembering more. "Then we got in the car and we left. We didn't even go into the house. And you were pregnant with Rosy – I remember that, too. You had her that night, in that tiny hospital in the little town halfway to the city. The nurse let me sleep in the waiting room and got me dinner." He looked at his mother. "We ran away. Why?" His voice cracked and he could feel tears in his eyes. "It was perfect here, and beautiful and you took it all away. I remember you and my father, and you were happy. What happened!?"

His mother didn't look at him. Instead she looked at the man who was his father. "I couldn't bear to lose him. And the leaves and flowers, I...I thought that if I didn't take him then, I would lose him."

The man smiled slightly. "We had a bargain, you and I. The first-born would be mine, and the second yours. You tried to cheat and have them both."

Tim looked at first one and then the other of his parent with alarm. He saw his sister doing the same.

Their father continued more gently. "You loved it here, and you loved me. We could have had everything together. Instead you tried to have it all for yourself." He shook his head sadly. "You couldn't, you know. Timothy has been mine from the day he was born, no matter where you took him. And now he is an adult, and he has come home to me." He paused again, and then, finally, he said softly, "We need to let them go, to lose them, as they grow up anyway. It is the inexorable way of nature and time."

Tim could feel something stirring inside him, the same thing that he had always felt in the green places his mother tried to keep him away from. It was the same thing he had felt the day of the leaves and lilacs.

The wind came up, and as the sun began to set, the clearing grew dusky. The man who was his father - and his sister's too, although she had never met him – began to change slightly. His eyes grew dark and rich as peat soil and vines wound up and over his shoulders. A bird lit on his head, which was suddenly shaggy and curly. His bare feet were tough-looking and his skin tanned and rough. His smile remained merry, but was less tame-looking. He reached out a hand and a wild rose bush grew up out of the ground and flowered.

He spoke again to Timothy's mother, "You lost so much. You have lost love, and time, and joy, and a life you would never have regretted, and all to no avail. Timothy is mine, as he always has been, despite all of your efforts." Hurt crossed his face, and he asked, "Did you not love me? Did I ever hurt you? Did I ever treat you with anything other than respect and love? I could not live within walls, but I gave you all that I could otherwise. I loved you will all of my heart. How could you leave me alone?" He shook his head slowly. "Never mind. I felt it that day, and I feel it now. The fear. As long as I seemed human, it did not rear its ugly head. But when you truly realized that there was more than what you could see, you felt the fear and you let it master you and you ran. Did you really think that seeing more would make me, and you, and our love, and our children, any different than we and they ever were?"

He turned to Tim and, as the wind whooshed into the clearing, he smiled sadly at his son. Tim smiled back, feeling the change in himself, knowing his life was changing right then and there. He looked down at his hands and felt the power of nature coursing through them as he had on his seventh birthday fourteen years ago in this very clearing.

Tim heard his mother sob and his sister's sounds of fear. If only they knew – there was nothing to fear. This was the most wonderful feeling he had ever had in his life. He was complete in a way that he had never been in the city.

They all stood there as it grew darker out. Lightning flashed in the distance. Finally Tim's mother said, "It is what it is. I can't deny what you said, and the truth is that I still love you. But I was so afraid of what might happen, of losing the son that I loved more than life itself. And now that time of our lives is over, and can't be changed." She hung her head as tears flowed down her cheeks. "Regret is a terrible, hopeless thing. Timothy, think of me now and then, and remember that I did what I did because I loved you. Rosy, let's go home." She took Rose's hand to draw her back down the path.

Then the forest-man spoke again. "Our daughter is yours, as we agreed. But I have been deprived of the chance to know my daughter, my Rose, and I will have it. So you have lost her, too, in return for the years you took Timothy away from me. I will take only seven years, although you stole fourteen." He turned to face her coldly. "You have made your choice, and in your greed, you have lost everything."

He reached out a hand to the now-sobbing Rose and gently drew her towards himself and Timothy. Their mother cried brokenly. She knew what she had done, knew the result was all her own fault.

Their father spoke. "Timothy, take your sister to the cabin and make her comfortable. You will need to stay with her for a while, I think; she is too young to stay alone and I cannot sleep within walls. But tomorrow, we will begin anew to know each other, and I will teach her this world as I taught you, until she is one and twenty. Help your mother down the path. I do not think she can see through the tears."

He watched them walk away, the plants parting for Timothy as he walked along, bowing to the new forest-lord. He shook his head at the broken woman who had carried his children, his heart breaking for all that she had lost, and knowing that she would still not see the choice in front of her. She would return to the city and mourn all that she had lost, and always wonder how it could have been different.

Then he whispered, a sound barely heard in the rustle of the breeze, "And if you wish to visit, we will rejoice with you." Whether or not she heard it was up to her.

MAPLE DAYS

Olivia sat hunched, head on knees, on the pedestal of the old statue in a little used corner of the park. She was a sad little figure, dressed all in black, with a too large black sweater hanging over her black t-shirt in acknowledgement of the chilly damp autumn twilight. It was clearly second or third hand and its snags and light spots attested to its previous owners' lack of care. A black beanie sat on her sandy hair, whose ends still showed evidence of an amateur attempt with black hair dye a few months back. The stone pedestal was damp, and it soaked through the tight black jeans she wore. She was so lost in her misery that she never noticed.

"Bunk over, Livvy, and make us some room," a voice nearby whispered.

Olivia didn't move, except for the heaving of her shoulders.

A finger dug into her hip. "Come on, scooch over!"

Her bottom moved over infinitesimally, but it was enough for the speaker to perch beside her.

"What's up, Liv? The idiots givin' you a hard time again?"

Olivia still didn't answer, and the two figures sat in silence for a while. Then the newcomer tried again.

"Say, Liv, you ready to come with me now? I've told you, I'll keep you safe, an' there'll be others there, like you. It'll be good. You know it will."

A tear splashed down on the damp stone between Olivia's legs.

"Hey, stop that, Skink! You know better than that!" Another voice came from the other side of the statue, and a head bobbed into view.

"Ah, buzz off, Maple. You don't have any business being here!"

"Do too. Olivia's my friend, too, Skink. In fact, she's known me longer than she has you!"

"Yeah, but where you been the last few years when things've been rough, huh? It's been me that's mostly been at her side, not you! So mind your own business and get lost!"

"Make me!"

"ENOUGH!" shouted Olivia, her head coming off her knees and her tear-streaked face glaring at the two on either side of her.

The second party sat down on the other side of Olivia, after sticking her tongue out at her rival.

"I don't need to listen to the two of you fight! I get enough of that at home and at school. So just shut up!" The head descended to the knees again with a sniffle. The three of them sat in silence for a while more, and then Maple spoke.

"Olivia, is there anything we can do to help?"

Olivia's head turned to the side and she looked at her friend. "No. You're here, and that's something. The rest of it, well, there's no help for it. Any of it."

Skink spoke up. "Just come with me, Livvy, and I promise you won't regret it!"

"Skink..." began Maple.

"No, it's okay Maple, I know better. Going with Skink would just be causing me new problems. Running away doesn't fix things." Olivia softened her words with a small smile at Skink, who hung his head slightly in acknowledgement of the truth of her words.

Silence reigned once more, and a yellow leaf floated down and stuck to the damp stone foot beside Olivia. A few raindrops leaked out of the sky. Finally Olivia heaved a sigh and leaned back against the legs of the statue.

"Tony found my notebook today. He took it and was looking at it in English class. Then Mrs. Thomson saw it and took it away. She kept it."

"Does she know it's yours?" asked Maple.

"Yeah. It has my name in the front. Now she's gonna read it. I don't know what she'll think. All I know is someone has my notebook and I want it back. I can't even write this evening 'cause I don't have another one." She sniffed loudly.

"There's no place for poets in your world, Olivia, especially poor ones from the wrong part of town," said Skink.

"So tell me something I don't know," she snorted.

Maple spoke up. "That's what Skink says. I don't know. He might be wrong. Just because your folks don't understand and the other kids don't get it, doesn't mean they speak for everyone. I see people writing all the time." Her face grew nostalgic. "I remember your mother writing."

Olivia smiled at her oldest friend, holding a precious image in her mind. She was about four years old, and had insisted her mother dress her in a poppy red dress to match Maple's bright clothing. They had been running around the park together, chasing autumn leaves in dancing the wind and laughing as Olivia's mother looked on with her eyes sparkling. Mother had understood, had known Maple and all of the others. She had never told Olivia to grow up and stop imagining things. It was all part of her world, too.

Mother and Olivia had told each other stories and played games and loved each other until the day Olivia had come home from kindergarten and found the fire truck and policemen at her building. They took her to another family that night, and then later on, another. She had been with this family for three years now, the longest she had been anywhere since Mother had died in the fire seven years ago. They weren't bad to her, just busy with lots of kids, some of whom had problems a lot worse than hers. They just weren't very understanding. Olivia had found this statue and Skink hiding near it one day when she was escaping the harried household.

Olivia reached out a gentle hand to Maple and her friend climbed on and then jumped to sit on Olivia's shoulder, her wings ticking Olivia's cheek.

Skink leaned against her, his gnarly little hand patting her foot gently. "Well, whenever you decide you want to come with me, you just let me know. I'll take you Underhill faster than you can say Robin Goodfellow. There's always a place for poets among the Gentry."

"Yeah, Skink, but I've read the stories. Humans don't do well there. They go crazy, or they stay there for a day that's a hundred years here. I don't want to do that and I don't want to be some kind of fancy pet for the elves. No thank you. Not now and probably not ever." Olivia curled one hand gently around Skink.

She spoke again. "If I could go anywhere, I'd go to my mother's mother. She was wonderful, my mother said. She wrote poetry, too - mother used to say some of it to me. And we had a picture she drew that looked a lot like you, Maple."

Maple and Skink were familiar with this story. "But you don't know where she is. The fire in the apartment that killed your mother burned anything that might have had her name on it, and no one has heard from her since." Maple began.

Skink took over, "And she wouldn't have known where to look for you, because your mother had had an argument with her and hadn't talked to her for a long time."

Olivia nodded. "Since before I was born. But she kept saying she was going to take me to see her, soon. And I know she was, because she bought two bus tickets, only I can't remember where to. I was so little then." Olivia sat lost in the past for a while and then jumped a little. It was nearly dark, and she was going to get in all kinds of trouble if she didn't get home right away. Bidding her friends a hasty good-bye, she raced off through the park to the apartment she shared with her foster parents and the other foster children.

When she got there, one of the other children met her at the door and told her to go to the living room. Her foster parents were sitting and waiting for her, along with Mrs. Thomson, who had Olivia's notebook in her hands. Olivia almost turned and ran back out the front door. She had been writing in class and not paying attention, but she hadn't thought it was a big enough deal for the teacher to come and visit. She crept quietly into the room and stood there with her head held high. She wouldn't let them get her down. She waited soundlessly for the lecture about wasting time with foolishness instead of studying.

Mrs. Thomson spoke first. "Olivia, I believe this notebook is yours?"

Olivia nodded silently.

"I looked at it. I'm sorry, because I know it's a private thing for you, but you brought it to school and I needed to see what was in it." She paused for a moment. "I'm glad I did look at it," she added.

Olivia winced, waiting for the rest.

"Olivia, these are very good. Very, very good. You have a real gift for poetry. The stories are well done, too, and I love the little drawings. Do you have any more?" Her face lit up as she asked.

Olivia stood there open-mouthed. Mrs. Thomson liked her foolish little poems and stories? Well, she had never thought they were foolish herself, but others had told her they were, so she had stopped letting people read them a long time ago. Slowly, she nodded and answered Mrs. Thomson's question. "I have a lot of notebooks. I keep them put away, though, 'cause the other kids think they're silly." She didn't add that the adults thought so too.

151

Mrs. Thomson nodded. "Other children can be harsh, I know." Olivia noticed her foster parents flushing slightly.

Her foster mother spoke up. "Do you really think there's any point to this? I mean, writing things isn't going to get her an education or a good job like studying hard and getting good grades, is it?"

Mrs. Thomson looked at them. "I understand why you want Olivia and the other children you care for to do well in school, but this could actually be to her advantage. Even now... There's a children's poetry competition for the city's schools. The winner gets a savings bond and a scholarship to City College whenever they are old enough to use it. Even the runners-up get savings bonds. This could actually be everything you want for Olivia."

Her foster parents looked stunned. "And you think Olivia's poetry is good enough to win?"

"I've seen the entries in past years. Yes, I think it is." She turned to Olivia. "Olivia, will you trust me enough to get some of your other books? I want to read through your work, and then you and I can choose the best one to submit for the competition. It closes next week, so we need to hurry."

Olivia stood there for a minute, unsure. Then behind her foster parents, on the window sill, she saw Maple. Maple was nodding and smiling. "Okay. Just a minute. I'll go and get them." The books were buried in the trunk where she kept all the things that were really hers, like the stuffed cat that had been saved from the apartment after the fire, along with her one picture of her mother and her grandmother. As she hurried off, she heard her foster parents discussing the contest details with Mrs. Thomson.

When she returned a little while later, with a stack of black hardbound composition books cradled in her arms, her foster parents were looking at her as if they were seeing her for the first time. "Olivia, we had no idea..." began her foster mother.

"We're sorry. We just didn't know." Her foster father said.

Olivia nodded and then she turned to Mrs. Thomson. "Can I have the newest one back? I don't have another one, and I want to do some more writing."

"Don't worry about that. I've got one you can have. I got too many when I was doing back to school shopping, and I think you need one of those now," said her foster mother.

Olivia watched nervously as Mrs. Thomson took the things that mattered the most to her away into the night.

Later that week, they chose the poem to submit. It was a poem called "Maple Days" that Olivia had written about that special day in the park with her mother, playing with Maple while her mother watched. Mrs. Thomson said it was a wonderful, special poem.

Olivia figured that even if it didn't win, at least people weren't laughing at her now, and she could write in peace as long as she got her school work done, too.

But she did win. The poem, along with her picture and name, were posted in the city newspaper, which had readers all over the state. The savings bond went in a special savings account, and the plaque that said she had won the scholarship went on the wall by her bed. Maple and Skink celebrated with her at the park. Maple in particular was delighted that Olivia had won because she was in the poem.

Things were getting back to normal again when the next surprise came.

Olivia came home from school one day to find her social worker in the living room. This was usually not the best thing - all too frequently it meant she was being moved, and she was as happy here as she had been anywhere since her mother died.

"Olivia, come here and sit down beside me," said the social worker. "I have some news for you."

Olivia warily came over and sat down.

"Olivia, when you won that poetry contest, you know that your name and picture were in the paper, as well as the poem."

Olivia nodded. She had several copies of the paper and the clippings put away in her trunk.

"Well, we had to wait to tell you until we were sure, but thanks to your win being published in the paper, we have found your grandmother. Or I should say, she found you." The woman smiled gently.

Olivia's heart leapt up into her throat.

"My grandmother?" she whispered.

"Yes, dear. And she had no idea what had happened to your mother, or to you. She feels terrible that you have had to do without each other for so long." The social worker went on to tell Olivia that her grandmother had noticed the picture first - Olivia apparently looked just like her mother had at her age. Her grandmother had known that Olivia had been born, but had not known her name or anything else about her, but since Olivia's mother had given Olivia a family name, that proved to be the second clue for her grandmother. Curious, her grandmother had done some investigating and found out about Olivia. She lived in a small town on the far side of the state, and she wanted Olivia to come and live with her. She was a school teacher.

Olivia sat there in shock. Her grandmother had found her, and wanted her. All of the stories her mother had told her came rushing back. She knew, even though her mother and grandmother had quarreled and her mother had left, that her grandmother was a good person who would love her just as she was.

"When can I meet her?" she whispered, tears rolling down her cheeks. She wiped them away with the sleeve of her black sweater.

"I'll bring her upstairs. She's waiting in the car."

Much later, when Olivia was settled in her grandmother's house, she and her grandmother were talking about how Grandmother had found Olivia.

"Your picture and your name were part of it, yes," Grandmother said as they sat by a warm fireplace in the book filled front room, "but the real clincher was the poem "Maple Days" itself. It was about Maple and while I didn't know your Maple, I know others of her kind. I knew that if you knew them, you must be my granddaughter." She smiled at Olivia with a smile so like Mother's that Olivia almost cried.

Olivia smiled back at her, and they both chuckled as Skink slipped out from behind the sofa and climbed up on the sofa beside them to try to cadge some popcorn.

ABOUT THE AUTHOR

Jane W. Wolfinbarger lives in Wyoming with her husband Pat, several Labrador retrievers, a large number of birds, enormous stacks of books and a yarn stash that threatens to take over any day now. She is the mother of four adult children and, in addition to writing, loves to read, knit, play with digital photography, and garden and ride her bike in the (very short Wyoming) summer.

You can visit Jane on Facebook at Jane W. Wolfinbarger, at her blog, janewwolfinbarger.wordpress.com, and on Twitter at JWWolfinbarger. You can email Jane at janewwolfinbarger@gmail.com.

Jane W. Wolfinbarger

CPSIA information can be obtained at www.ICGtesting.com
Printed in the USA
LVOW072105271112

309049LV00011BA/793/P